Faith

MALARKEY BOOKS
PO BOX 331
ASBURY MO 64832

Faith

A novel
Itoro Bassey

Malarkey Books

Published by Malarkey Books

Ebook available at the publisher's website:
Malarkeybooks.com

ISBN: 978-1-0879-9147-4

Typesetting by Alan Good

Cover Design by Angelo Maneage
angelomaneagethewebsite.com

To those who had no roadmap.

The Family Breakdown

Uduak: Mother
Dad/The father: The second husband
Uduak's mother: Grandmother
Uduak's grandmother: Great grandmother
Ekom: The first daughter
Arit: The second daughter
Okon: The only son
Ekpewan: Half-sister

Prologue

You see this thumb I have? It is my thumb. No one else in the world has this same thumb. It is my own to account for. The marks, the stretches, even the lines running through it, so dark and severe, are mine. When my Maker asks what I did with this thumb I carried into my old age, there will be no one to answer for me but myself.

When you die, they will bury you alone. No one else will go in there with you. It's not allowed. You hear? It's your Maker. Your voice. And that voice follows you into the very dark of your grave and this is the true judgment day, when your body is laid to rest, as they heap the earth on you and plant you as if you were a seed.

The voice that follows you knows the dreams you dreamt in your slumber but never acted on when awake. It has within it the sound of you, but if you think it will forgive your shortcomings, then you don't understand this voice. It will hand you the sum of your creation or the lack of your creating and then you will hear a cry, and that is the cry of a spirit being born. That spirit travels back to the earth to realize their own dreams and make sense of your failures. Get it?

Life is a dance of humans traversing in and out of worlds, until the Maker says you have done what you need to do. With constant change, it is guaranteed that worlds will collide. So I ask you now, what spirit will you grow?

Part 1

Start now. Start where you are.
Start with fear. Start with pain.
Start with doubt. Start with hands
shaking. Start with voice
trembling but start. Start
and don't stop. Start where you are,
with what you have. Just . . . start.

—Ijeoma Umebinyuo

Running
The United States, 1995-2014. Arit.

I've got an ancestor on my back.

She wades through whatever spirit-filled world she inhabits to rest herself beside me while I sleep. She notices every inane habit of mine, down to the crease that forms between my brows when I frown. *What makes you different?* Her knobby fingers wriggle between mine, and she positions her mouth next to my ear. *A language? A country? A history? A prayer? I wanted to be you.* Everything I eat. Wear. Say. Think. Sing. Love. Hate. She knows.

I'm from your mother's side. I died about a four-hour drive from her hometown. Her people go to church and rest on the street with that half-built apartment where the workers drill but never finish the job. I visited them often in the summers with my aunt. They're still over there. Living and waiting.

She sniffs out my trail, watching to see if anything she says will finally click. These people—she claims—wear the same face and frown that I do. I haven't seen them since I was two or three, and I may never see them again. No one speaks their names over here unless one of them dies, so if they haven't died, I haven't heard of them.

Possibly, my mother mentioned these people when talking about the good old days. Like that time she was driving and talked about her girlhood days of getting water from a river with her cousins. Perhaps they were the dearly loved cousins in those pictures I saw in our family scrapbook. They walked four miles to a river they called "Nature's Mirror" because it was so clear you could see all of nature in it. It's polluted now. Crumpled papers, empty soda bottles, plastic bags, and food scraps now litter her memory of swimming in that river. No one takes good care of it anymore, I guess. I'll never get to see the river through her eyes, that's for sure.

When she told me that story, I barely listened. All I could think about was her driving fast enough to get me to the winter dance while I checked my cherry lip gloss and frosted eyeliner in the mirror. Her foot pressed the brake every thirty seconds to ensure we wouldn't skid off the road, and my only thoughts were of my failed attempt at beauty: despite my best efforts, I was sure no one would pick me to dance. If I had grown up in her country, I wouldn't have been so distracted and afraid, and could've heard her story of a clear river with laughing cousins. But I've put too much of myself into surviving on *this* land, and if there's a story I need, it's about making life work out here. I blame the country this ancestor and my mother speak of for my parents birthing their children in a slush of desperation and fear. My anger at their homeland makes me quintessentially American; I never ask what happened to their people or country. I only consider the fruit their country produced: the unforgiving faces and disjointed actions of my parents. And that, I can't forgive. I'm an American through and through. At least, I hope I am. Americans like me don't bother to factor ourselves into the equation of any culpability. There'd be too much explaining and heartache that way.

The ancestor resting beside me sniffs out my sentiments in the way I roll my eyes and scoff at her talk of this so-called family waiting for me in another country. *You were very little when you visited. You wanted to play games nobody knew or cared to understand, so I left you sitting on the couch and took your sister to play instead. She was old enough and the games we played were games we understood. I should have spent more time with you. Maybe if I were nicer then you would have liked to visit.* Her breath heats the tip of my ear.

There's nothing to forgive because I can't remember a thing about a thing. She's telling the truth though, this much I know, because in the family photo album I see myself, a little girl with beads in her hair and a scowling face staring at the camera, surrounded by people. They stare at the camera with scowling faces too, some dressed in school uniforms, head wraps or tunics, one little boy in a buttoned-up checkered shirt with his hand on my shoulder, confident by that subtle gesture that we are kin. Their eyes stretch across their faces as mine do. Are these the people waiting for me to visit? Surely the spirit knows we've moved on from those pictures. I have a little brother they've never seen, and we've grown taller and gained weight while the photo album gathers dust on a bookshelf. Those people should stop waiting, and this ancestor should move on to her next life because if she's dead I think that having a family must not have been that great. Besides, her photo isn't in the family album. Who is this ancestor to me?

She recounts stories of her adventures roaming different worlds. Where she goes, she can ride on the back of a sound and join spirits with dancing feet and swaying hips. These spirits, she tells me, were once humans and they now dance to a vibration sitting between wailing and praise. *We dance away our sadness to make up for our hard time on earth.*

One time, she traced my nose with her fingers. *When I come back to earth, I come back to learn, it's like school.*

"Take me with you!" I said, jumping in excitement because the spirit lit an interest in me. "I like to dance."

She rubbed her knee, a knee as knobby as her fingers. *Anyone can dance for an eternity, but to live here on earth, that's not a task for the weak-willed. You, my dear, are stronger than me.*

Another time, she visited me on a bad night. Bad nights consist of me hiding in my room while trying to scream into a pillow. Hearing the muffled sounds of my voice frightened me, and I shuddered realizing that nearly everything made me jumpy. Dad had caused a row about the trash and when Mom came home, she plopped two large steak-and-cheese subs with extra jalapeños and mayo on the table and then bolted to sleep. The covers were over her head when I leaned over the bed to hug her. I couldn't say much, and neither could she, just a muttered: "You must respect your father." I inhaled half my sub with orange Fanta thinking that I better put myself in the can for trash collection next week. But then it dawned on me that creatures of a gross sort would crawl on me. If there were millipedes, I wouldn't last a minute. Millipedes were a bounty in my yard, and they'd slink into the house, so they'd slink into a trash can no doubt.

When the spirit arrived, I didn't tell her that I was happy to see her, I just asked, "Can I go with you?"

She cupped my face in her hands. *No, dear.*

I punched her, though my punches didn't hit skin or bone, it was more like punching air or trying to hold water.

I won't take you anywhere until you are too old to be alive.

I lunged at her, hoping to pinch her nose till she cried, but she curled into herself and vanished. I lay there all night thinking, sometimes, you've got to keep punching until a bone cracks beneath your fist.

She first appeared when I turned ten. I was too much of a wuss to leave home, but I thought about it. I sulked in my room, trying to hide from the feast Mom was cooking. The palm oil heating on the stove seeped through the cracks of my door and coated my nostrils, causing me to sneeze. I could hear laughter from my sister and brother over a preacher's voice blaring from the television, speaking of God and salvation. I was grateful that my door muffled the sounds of the I'm-gonna-get-saved music playing after the preacher's sermon. When the TV evangelist's voice thundered and Mom cooked while humming a hymn or a prayer, it was a good night.

About half an hour later, someone yelled from the bottom of the steps, "Come down and eat!" Since I was the only one puttering around upstairs, the decree was for me. I was a hiding kind of kid. Hid from the Gospel. Hid from appeals they sent to the Most High invoking my name, hid from her crooning, hid from his footsteps, hid from their laughter, hid from kids at school chanting "she's too blacky black," hid from report cards inked in red with C+ next to three out of five subjects, and vigilantly hid from the kitchen, the unofficial town square of every household. I hid until I forgot.

That night I hadn't been called to help cook, and I sat on my bed cursing the smell invading my privacy. Would it be so wrong to eat spaghetti or a tuna casserole? Not that my parents ever made casseroles, but could they at least try to make one? That's what most kids at my school ate for dinner.

That night I ate spinach soup with doughy Bisquick, wishing a wormy string had slid down my throat. A couple of hours later, the ancestor girl woke me from my sleep. She sat next to my bed, picking the crust from the corners of my eyes.

Her head was shaved, revealing large oval eyes that left little room for a nose and mouth. She bragged about her hair growing quick and thick, *quick thick.* She shaved it twice a month to adhere to the school rules that girls must keep their hair low. That's how she spoke of it, keep the hair low. *It's so we'll focus on being smart. I still want to be smart so my hair doesn't grow well. I've been told it'll grow once I start feeling better about things.* My hair's like Mom's, fine and easily breakable. I told her this, not thinking it was such a big deal, but she was dissatisfied with this response. *You're blessed. You know your mother and that means you know something about yourself.*

She liked quizzing me for sport. It was like a dodgeball game, her throwing blows, gleeful that I wouldn't catch a single ball. *Oh, you can't make jollof? But that's so simple, nau?* I could see her nicking off points from the scorecard, happy that she disgraced me to the bleachers. But I was already defeated, playing wisecrack games with a dead girl. She could walk through walls and ogle you with your pants down and you'd be none the wiser. The final laugh was hers.

"All mothers are strangers to their children and I don't need to know how to make rice." I flung her anger back to her side of the court and saw that fiery light in her dim. Being alive gave me an edge. "She married twice," I offered. "Her first husband was mean."

"No, you have it wrong. No person can be mean all the time," she said.

"Yes they can. Look at my dad."

"You don't know him then. Every mean person has a day when they laugh and a night when they cry."

"I don't believe you."

"Doesn't matter if you don't. It's the truth."

"Well then the truth is mean."

"Aha! Now you're getting it. So tell me something more about your mum . . ."

If it would have made her happy, I'd have marched her downstairs to Mom and announced, "Let me introduce you to this spirit in search of a mother, because apparently when you die it's likely that you'll gripe over your mommylessness and find a human to whine to about it. You're free to take this lost soul off my hands and add another mouth to feed at the table. She believes you're the right person for the job, and lucky for you there's no red tape you gotta go through to get her. Good day."

The ancestor must have been around seventeen or eighteen because she talked like someone who was ready to go out into the world on her own terms, but her shaved head made her look younger, like a thirteen- or fourteen-year-old. She wore a long dress that was lined with plain white buttons trailing down the middle. If she dared come to my school dressed like that the kids would point and laugh. Even the *uncool* kids would point and laugh. If I had seen her walking through the hallways like that, I may have pointed and laughed, or pretended we weren't related.

She rubbed my cheek and wiped the drool off my chin. Then she turned to a plate of spaghetti and meatballs sitting on her lap. The plate looked exactly like what I had craved for dinner. She let the noodles dangle from the fork as she took a bite. *It tastes okay. Soon you'll see that it's not the best.*

I dismissed her visit thinking she was nothing but a pestering dream, but her touch on the side of my eyes and chin left a tingle on my face that lingered the entire weekend.

A few days later she caught me on another bad night. It was a day when the evangelist preacher wasn't blaring from the television. Mom was asleep, and we children made lunch and dinner for ourselves, eating ramen noodles, chocolate chip cookies (the chewy kind), and leftover soup with rice. We watched morning cartoons turn to family-friendly afternoon movies to R-rated night shows with kissing girls and boys we weren't supposed to watch. That day the TV shows bored me, and I decided to have some fun in my room.

In my room, I danced, sang, and pretended to date a guy named John with blow-in-the-wind hair. I drew pictures of what I would look like in the future. My future-self looked like a tall woman with large hoop earrings and a back that didn't hunch. Her mouth was closed and though she'd never say it, I knew she was not afraid. I'd turn on the radio and dance to the latest pop and R&B tunes. I let my body stomp and twirl in the room, doing a liturgical dance to the future. In my merriment, I jumped as if trying to fly across town, the state, or the country until I sweated. When I danced this way, trouble usually followed me upstairs. In my room I learned that trouble always followed if I danced to wish for something different.

He never knocked on the door, and the lock to my room never worked. He entered that day, giving me no time to bring myself back to reality.

"Didn't you hear me calling you?" he asked.

"Yes," I muttered. That was a grave mistake. You just don't answer "yes" when a parent calls you. You must address adults according to their position and title; I should have said, "Yes, Daddy." He hit me over the head for that one, and I fell back on the bed with the left side of my head throbbing.

"Why are you so rude?" He raised his arm ready to strike again, but my feet started to kick the way they did when I danced and twirled in my room. He tried to find a limb to grab, but my legs kicked till I couldn't see them anymore. I gained momentum like a fan once it's turned on, and I kicked until he turned to leave.

I had won, but I knew once I went downstairs I'd pay for my disobedience. I played music and danced till I fell asleep.

That night the spirit visited again. *So you all kick your fathers over here? Siii!*

I turned away to the wall, but then she appeared lying next to me, with her broad forehead pressed against mine. "If you were me, you'd kick him too," I said.

You should stop doing that. It is wrong for daughters to kick their fathers. The ancestor took her forehead off mine and scowled, like the way those people in the pictures scowled in the family photo album.

"Is it wrong for fathers to hit their daughters?" I asked.

She scanned my face. I could tell she wanted to answer but she just sucked her teeth. *Why do you hide away from your family?*

That night, I told her about all the things I heard from my room. Chairs thudding against the wall. Someone crying. Parents bickering in a language I didn't speak. Occasional laughter and giggles, but mostly an overbearing preacher and gospel music playing from the family TV.

I told her about what happened in the house when I left the room. I told her about how each time I went downstairs, my chest tightened and my knees began to hurt. I told her the story about the time I saved my life before I had to eat dinner. I was washing a dish to eat with, and I must have done something to make him angry with me. When I turned around, I saw him with a softball in his hand. That was the softball my sister used to practice for her

23

games, games that for some reason I never got to see. I couldn't explain to the spirit how he found the softball lying around in the kitchen. But that's the way it was in our house. You'd see a softball placed next to a fork, a bag of Cheetos, and a can of Raid.

I watched him pick up the softball and aim it towards my forehead. Thankfully, something in my body reacted and my arm came up to block the collision from happening. I figured that if I was going to get out alive, I'd need to have my head intact. He tried to strike once more, and I wrapped my arms around my head. Finally, he got tired of me covering my head and stomped away. It wasn't until he left that I realized the rest of the family was watching from the dinner table. We looked at each other, blinking for a moment or two until there was nothing to do but laugh.

"Sorry," Mom said after a wave of laughter. "That would have been real bad if he had hit you."

"Yeah, that softball was coming for your head pretty fast," my sister added.

I sat down with my dish, and we went on eating.

"That's why I hide," I told the ancestor.

She rubbed my cheek. *I wanted to be you.*

I told her we could switch bodies. I assumed she had the power to make that happen. Dancing and flying between heaven and earth seemed like a treat. Maybe I wouldn't mind wearing a long dress with plain buttons. She could take my life and have my body any day of the week. But she didn't seem interested in switching bodies, all she wanted to do was ask me questions.

She asked if I knew the language my parents spoke, and I told her the words I learned. Amesiere meant good morning, didiamkpo meant come and eat, dimi meant come here, and kopinwa meant shut up. Tears fell down her face onto her dress. I tried to wipe a tear away, but my hand just went through her.

"Are you dead?" I asked.

She sucked her teeth and sat up in bed. *They buried my body in a grave, and I believe they gave me a tombstone.*

I tried putting my hand in hers, but it just went through her, and I finally stopped trying to touch her because I realized she wasn't made of bone or flesh. That night I learned two things about her: her mother sent her away when she was a baby, and she never got to visit America like she had hoped.

If I'm in my room, Dad won't hit me because he thinks I practice juju upstairs. Mom knocks before entering, and my brother and sister make fun of me from outside the door. They chuckle saying, "She's talking to herself again," or, "She's jumping around again," or, "One of these days she's gonna break the floor." They say I'm bizarre. They don't know that sometimes the ancestor dances with me. I taught her how to do the butterfly and tootsie roll. I draw pictures of what she could look like in the future, and she insists that I draw her in jeans and a tube top. I still say, "Yes, Daddy," eat what's on the table, and say my prayers.

One time, Dad entered without knocking to hand me a book called *The Souls of Black Folk.* All I knew was that the book was thick and the author looked like he broods all day. What did I care about the souls of Black folk for? Dad teaches Africana Studies as an adjunct professor at a community college and loves books.

"They pay pennies," he says, "but at least I'm not driving a taxi with degrees but no options." Dad takes a long shower, shaves his beard, and leaves the house whistling when it's time to teach. It's the only job he'll work without a fuss. He refuses to work at any place where he has to punch in and out on someone else's clock. In his words, those jobs are mindless, and he didn't come to America to languish in a dank room watching a machine stamp a high-class brand name into a knife.

His eyes inspected my room. "Your jumping better get you to Harvard."

I looked at the cover and guessed the book to be about five hundred pages or so.

"Read this and have an essay to me by the end of next week. You should know who this man is."

I was fifteen. I cared little for school, and even less for Harvard, though I read the books he gave me because I cared for my life. I went downstairs to sit at my mom's bedside and complain. She let out a small laugh.

"Read it. You all don't have my love for science, but you do have your father's love for words. Don't be like us with all these book smarts but no money coming in. Working retail is no joke, dear." She pulled the cover over her head and went back to sleep.

That night the schoolgirl visited me, rubbing my cheek and touching my braids. *Your mother really enjoys sleep. Why?*

I shrugged. She moved to take the latest book I must read off my desk. "It's so dumb I have to read that," I said.

She thumbed through the pages, making a few grunts and sighs, perhaps showing a little bit of curiosity for the book.

"It's alright," I said nonchalantly. "If you're into history it's an okay read. The author writes like he's too smart to say things plain because educated people like to talk too much, but all he's saying is that nothing that our teachers taught us in school about this country is true, and if you're Black you really can't afford to lie to yourself."

The spirit raised her eyes from the book and looked at me with a smirk on her face. *So your father isn't all that bad, huh?* She smiled almost wickedly, and in that moment I tried to ignore the gnawing thought telling me I hated her. *You will miss them when you leave here.* She put the book down. *When you finish reading, tell me everything. Don't hide good information o.*

That night I learned her name is Ekpewan.

It was my sixteenth birthday, and Ekpewan always visits on my birthday. For years that was our ritual. She'd arrive flushed and out of breath because she'd been dancing. Sweat would run from her forehead and she'd smile. *I dance over there the way you dance over here. I dance so we can find peace. Soon. soon. . .*

This birthday was different. I still was afraid to escape but I was old enough to know I would soon leave. I was also old enough to see that dancing and twirling in this world does not always mean things will change. I didn't need a spirit who couldn't help me traipsing around here. We needed a miracle. The snow-haired evangelist said if we believed and tithed more, we would get one. We gave ten percent to the church and kept the TV preacher speaking from morning till night, and still no miracle. Giving money to said preacher's church did not equal a miracle. For all the smarts my family said they had I didn't understand how they came to accept such a ridiculous equation as a fact. The only benefit I saw was our dollars and coins weighing heavy in the preacher's pocket while we kids continued to eat ramen noodles and stale bologna sandwiches for lunch. I was sixteen and thinking like a true American. Miracles aren't handouts, a true miracle is bought. The miracle is in the racketeer's pockets! I wanted to scream this at them. Take the velvet tithing basket and dump it into your purse. Pay your bills and get your miracle. You'll feel better waiting for God's light knowing your electricity won't shut off. I thought that to myself whenever I saw my mom's worn hands drop a check into the basket.

But if they were to follow me into my room and watch me when I shut the door, they'd find me entertaining a spirit. If they found out that my closest friend was a spirit that went to another world to dance, I'm not sure they'd say, "Now there goes a girl with her wits about her. Let's put our faith in her."

Maybe we're all untrustworthy in one way or another because if I said the words, *I speak to spirits* out loud, I wouldn't trust myself.

That birthday night I waited, sitting with the pillow against the wall, awake and ready. Ready to catch her. I couldn't tell if she flew through the wall, or door, or ceiling to get to me, but she appeared smiling. She always arrived like she never left, and it bugged me that I could never pinpoint how she entered my room. I straightened my back against the pillow and leaned forward, hoping my voice wouldn't crack. "Unless you can bring us a miracle, stop visiting." Before she could sit, I said these words.

She moved a bit closer, maybe wanting to rub my cheek or wipe a tear.

"You stay away, please. I gotta get out. I get what you're saying but you've got to understand what I'm saying too. They hurt me. I can't prove it. But it's happening."

She let out a tiny noise, but it wasn't a noise of anger, it was like a squeal she had to muffle so it would be easier to control. I shouldn't have been so startled, but it just didn't seem natural, but then again she was a dead girl. I had a suspicion that even though she had said nothing I had made a mistake.

This is how I did it. The night I sent her away, I knelt in front of my bed the way Mom had taught me to. I usually hated lowering my head before a man sitting somewhere in the sky. I had wasted enough of my life bowing down, counting the scratches in wooden floors, but this time it would be different.

"When you become a woman, you'll learn how to find comfort behind a locked door kneeling over your bed." Mom would tell me this whenever I'd frown in defiance of having to sing another praise song or fumble through reading Psalm 63 before I was allowed to sleep.

On my bed I remember you, I think of you through the watches of the night. Because you are my help, I sing in the shadow of your wings.

I had remained skeptical of sweaty evangelical preachers, and whether or not Moses parted the Red Sea with his staff, but that night I thrusted my arms back and forth ready to call on the God of my own making.

A wooden floor mirror stood at the side of my bed. I had always wondered why it was placed there. I had rationalized that the room was too small for it to fit anywhere else, but I wondered if it was there for me to start praying to myself. The God I wanted had a wide nose and skin that turned the color of eggplant when it was hot outside. She knew what it felt like to be chosen last for her PE class and understood what it was like to wish that the lock on your door actually worked. I didn't have much favor with a Santa Claus-like man dressed in a robe, but I could garner sympathy from the girl staring at me.

"Put me to sleep," I said. "I'd like not to feel so much, so turn the switch off. This is my prayer."

You wouldn't believe it but that girl in the mirror observed my blubbering quite mildly and said, *Continue.* She was intent in her focus, willing to hear my piece, and I wondered if love is the act of being impartial while you lend yourself to witnessing it all.

My stomach growled suddenly and then my mouth watered. I had a taste for sugar, a hankering for a drop of honey to coat the bitterness sloshing around like a paste in my mouth. And the tiny pricks! Those pricks nicking the corners of my stomach, reminding me that my guts needed satiating.

Mom screamed from the bottom of the stairs, "Didiampko!"

I would have normally turned the volume on my Walkman up, blasting Aaliyah in my ears, because it was probably okra soup she had made, or some kind of porridge, but that day I relinquished all protest.

"Be there in a minute," I said.

I call home twice a week. Sundays I call because my family goes to church, and it's rude for a daughter not to call her family after service. Wednesdays I call them because those are the days I must run to wash dishes between classes and homework.

From morning until dinner, I work shifts as a dishwasher, a gig I worked out with the financial aid office for work-study. I never see the faces of students placing their dirty plates in the dish trays. I do see their hands though. Hands with shiny rings, leather watches, magenta nails, all placing half-scraped dishes in trays and utensils in soapy water. I study the hands of those of us taking the dirty plates to wash. Our hands are the color of dusk, tree bark, squash, pearl, and hazelnut. Our hands spray half-eaten food off plates into the sink. Our hands are from the Dominican Republic, Los Angeles, Nicaragua, Ohio, Senegal, Massachusetts, New York, China, Mexico, Cambodia, Florida, and Barbados. My fingertips soak in the water so much they morph into tiny old women. Nothing but creases and veins that make me think of what a bucket of soapy warm water can reveal.

Some of us pulling the lever to turn on the dishwasher are the first in our families to walk these hallowed halls our parents took low-paying jobs to put us in. Some of us take the dishes with satisfaction, knowing we will have our time to duke it out with the decorated hands that give us their filthy plates. We'll be ready for those hands in class, knowing that soon enough we'll give them their dirty dish back.

When they ask why children from "underprivileged areas" never have their parents around, we'll say our parents are busy, busy washing the plates of people with shiny rings and watches. Busy scrubbing their toilets and wiping the asses of their ungrateful children. Then we'll say the things our parents couldn't say because they needed the money for us.

We also have other perks that come with our parents' hopes and prayers, like the luxury of hopping from one dining hall to another and swiping our ID cards that let us eat with wild abandon. The grumble in my belly isn't all-consuming like when I was home. There are other things to fill myself with, like staying up all night to write ten-page papers for my African American lit class or daydreaming about how I'll land a high-paying corporate job and drive a Mercedes Benz by the time I graduate.

From time to time, the gnawing chews my stomach and alerts me that I need a fix. My appetite has been expanded to life beyond buttercream frosting and Arnold Palmers. Our cards give us access to noodle-bowl nights, vegan yogurt, bagels with lox, and good old hamburgers with french fries. If our families travel to dine in these hallowed halls, they must pay to eat. Non-ID carriers must pay for the five-star cuisine the school offers. Sometimes they can pay, other times we take our Tupperware to the dining hall and stash extra food for our families. We also get to study abroad or cry in the college counselor's office when we're overwhelmed. No wonder when we visit home our arrogance prompts someone to ask, "Who are you?" But I think, look what a prestigious liberal arts college can do? It can lift you out of one life and into another and isn't this what we wanted?

On Wednesdays when my apron is soggy, I call home.

My parents still pray and give their ten percent to the church. My brother transferred to a new high school where the students are college bound and the class sizes are much smaller, which in layman's terms means he's at a predominantly white school with hapless teachers mispronouncing his name every chance they get. My sister's in her last year of college and is leading six different organizations while failing advanced calculus. And Dad, what to say of him? That man will scream into the void until he tires himself out and there'll be nothing to say but, Amen.

They're blood, and blood binds. It's familiar to dial their number, like brushing my teeth for the sake of not having garbage breath. I call so I don't lose them. Would be a shame to lose an entire family. If I can make Thanksgiving or Christmas, I'll try, but I have no money to buy gifts or contribute to food. If I want to see them for the holidays, I better pick up another gig polishing silver for the fancy dinners the college president hosts.

One night, after I called my Mom, I could tell the schoolgirl, Ekpewan, was around. She didn't reveal herself, and I didn't think I had the sensitivity to see her anymore anyway. Studying for exams replaced my days of dancing and drawing pictures of my future self. The tingle on my ear gave her away. I wasn't ready to see her, but I was willing to talk again. And listen. *If you leave them for good, who will you become?*

The next morning, I called Mom again. Her work schedule is more grueling than mine. She works during the day as an adjunct professor, and in the evening she works retail. On Sundays she's energized from the rush of hearing the Word and more willing to share a few good words of her own. During our Sunday phone calls, I learned that she was once a girl (a fact that shocked me, since I thought she came out of her mother an exhausted woman), believes there is God in science ("How can you look under the microscope and watch those cells move and not see the work of God?" she says), and never got around to truly understanding her grandma from her mother's side for reasons that shall remain unnamed (because since when does Mom ever go through the trouble of stating the reason?). She'll tell me stories about her mother and begins her sentences with, "My mother taught me . . ." or, "She was a wise woman." I think she tells me these things because she left her mother's house too, and maybe she didn't listen to anything her mother said until it was too late.

When she was a girl, she liked to devour mangos from a tree in her compound and chew the skins too, because the skins are where all the best nutrients are, don't you know, where her maids woke up with the roosters and swept the outside tiles, and then the family woke up for prayers because you ought to start every morning with a family prayer, thanking God for breath, thanking God for the sun, thanking God for jam with white bread, and all I can think is Lord this all sounds very sweet, but it's such a saccharine taste that I worry I'll throw up, because I don't believe anybody's life can be this good, certainly not hers anyway. I'd never dare say this out loud though, there are words a daughter should never say to her mother unless she's ready to become motherless in the world.

It was Thursday morning and I listened to Mom's sighs and murmurs of exhaustion. She had to finish prepping lessons for her classes and fix her mind on working a six-hour shift selling furniture and appliances.

"I love you," I said. "I love you very much."

The line was quiet, and I wasn't sure if I was hearing her breathe or if there was static on the other side.

"I love you too, dear," she replied, "and remember, God loves you most."

That night I lay awake in bed and prayed. I lay in bed, ready to talk about what I remembered. I whispered to myself, knowing a young girl with red eyes and eggplant skin was listening until I fell asleep.

Here, you must choose sides. In the land of the free and the home of the brave they couldn't care less whether you're Yoruba, Igbo, Ijaw, Galambi, Efik, Ibibio, Hausa, from the North or the South, multilingual, or the daughter of a chief. They don't care if you puke out the colors red, white, and blue, or love their founding fathers more than they do. When you go outside, they don't see your tribe, or the garb you so proudly choose to wear or not wear; they see skin.

"We're not far from the dark ages here," I told Ekpewan. "Here, your skin is currency."

When you're walking down the street, no one asks who you are, where you're from, where your people are from, whether you're rich or poor or somewhere fledgling in the middle, you're Black, and Black skin means you're a perpetual foreigner. Here, they shoot first and ask questions later, if they even ask them at all. I told this to Ekpewan.

She eavesdrops on conversations I have with friends, all of us Black women, with our legs and arms crisscrossed with one another so we can fit on my twin-sized bed. They're from Atlanta, Arkansas, and Pasadena. They've been born and reborn in this country for generations, much longer than I have. Lisa, my friend from Arkansas, told us about the high school sweetheart she left in the South.

"Down there, white folks can laugh with you over a glass of lemonade, but the next day they'll call you a nigger if you step out of place. They'll laugh with you till they're beet red so long as you know they're white and you're Black. When I started dating Bryant, his parents kicked him out of the house for a week. They wanted him to stay at his grandparents' house, but his grandparents didn't want to take him in, so he had to stay at his uncle's place in the next town. His dad went to see him and had a 'good ole boy' talk with him, saying that before he got married, he also had a case of 'jungle fever' before settling down to a respectable life. His dad was like, 'I'll let you back in the house because this is gonna end.' Can you believe that?"

One of the women rolled her eyes and let out a sigh before giving an answer. "Well, after listening to white people say they're not racist after wearing blackface for Halloween . . . it definitely is within the realm of possibility."

Ah-ah! The whites like to paint their faces Black over here? But why!? Ekpewan. She always interjects into our conversations. I hoped she didn't reveal herself and scare my friends away. They'd run out of here so fast. We giggled, letting our arms and legs shake with our laughter. I suspected Ekpewan might have found a little space on the bed, or sat leaned over in a chair, laughing too.

"Why would Bryant tell you this?" I asked.

"'Cause he felt guilty, like they always do when they know they're not gonna do shit. He said he was in love with me and wanted to get married. The Southern girl in me said, 'of course I'll marry you,' but if I wasn't even allowed in his house, how would we work out? We didn't last too long after that."

Ekpewan's voice stayed with me throughout the day, following me into the shower, my classroom, dinner, and bedtime because she was bent on understanding the conversations I had with my friends. *These friends you have are good. They have guts. You need guts to live on earth. But what about your other sisters I see walking on campus, the ones coming from Africa? You never sit with them. Why?*

I murmured back to her while turning towards the wall, "I don't know my language, I don't talk much to my parents, and I can't stand the Nigerian gospel songs they play."

What does that have to do with saying hello and eating lunch with somebody? Though I couldn't see her, I guessed she was lying next to me, tracing my nose with her finger, or moving about the room dancing.

"Let me break it down for you." I pulled myself upright in bed. "The Africans and Caribbeans don't cross into the Black Student Union, and Black Americans don't really cross into the African & Caribbean Association. Sometimes we'll go to each other's dances or movie nights, but overall, we stay in our lanes. One side thinks the other is lucky to be in America because their homelands are barbaric and their cultures need to be modernized, and the other side thinks the other is lazy, and they don't want to be guilty by association when they get here, so . . . it's easier not to associate."

And what of you? she challenged, as if wagering a bet to see if I was quick enough to match her appraisal. *Are you not African?*

"I was born here," I snapped. "As far as I know, I'm American-made." She did not say anything after my thorough explanation. I felt a tickle of satisfaction, triumphantly lying back in bed. I outranked her somehow because I understood something more than she did.

That night, a dream came. Or perhaps something more like a memory. In the dream, I was dancing with my siblings and some distant cousins that came to visit us from Connecticut. The fact that we moved into a three-story house was cause for a party. I must have been eight or nine. One of the aunties brought dollar bills to shower the children with while we danced. I remember grabbing the floating bills and dancing to some song with a good beat. In the dream, I had more time to observe the smiles forming while we danced, and hear my parents say something about spraying us with money on our wedding day. The next morning, I woke up and wrote about everything I remembered about my life before I left home. I was ready to talk frankly to the God I saw in the mirror that night.

To the God who looks like me,

I used to get hit and called a lot of names at home. My dad would say I was a crafty kid and a fool. My mom stood by and watched him. Don't know what to make of her, but a friend I met in one of my classes said that in a household like mine, the man always wins. She's from Cameroon. But you got me out of that place, so now I'm asking you to help me again, because when I graduate I don't want to live with my parents. I don't know where I'll go if I don't go home, but make it somewhere nice.

I want a high-paying job, and a Mercedes in a nice neighborhood where people walk dogs with silly names like Periwinkle. Take me to California where there's no snow and the weather's nice. Help me put this degree to good use. Let it buy me some comfort. After all, I go to a good college and we're supposed to be the leaders and the voices of the future. So then give me a big voice with a lot of money. Didn't we come here to attain this? So then gimme that. Gimmie all of that.

Yours,

Arit

On Sundays, I clean my apartment. I begin with my room, going through the closet to find unworn sweaters and pants I swore I'd wear months ago. If it turns out the hangers wore a shirt or pair of itchy jeggings more than I did, those clothes go in a box for donation. Then, I clean the bathroom, scrubbing

41

the floor, toilet, and tub till I see their surfaces glisten. My mom said the two cleanest places in a home should be the kitchen and the bathroom. So I sweep every corner, mop as far under the refrigerator as the Swiffer will let me, and polish my forks and spoons until I see myself in everything I've touched.

I live on a street where people walk under bright umbrellas when the sun gets too hot. Police cars speed down the street during the day, and during the night they speed down the street with their bells and whistles ringing. When you walk further down, you'll see bright walking umbrellas change to people hanging on the corners or sauntering across the road, letting cars swerve around them while drivers honk out their frustration. Selena's bidi-bidi-bombom blasts onto the street, giving people a bit of nostalgia for a woman wearing a bustier with silver sequins, unafraid to sing the songs of a resilient people. One week, a 90s R&B girl group blared from someone's storefront, causing a passerby to yell to the owner, "Man, you're playing all the slaps out here!" A stocky man with a baseball cap sells bags of cut watermelon and mango with chili and lime juice on the street to people on their way to the bus, to the hospital, to the store, to their homes.

When I finish cleaning my studio, I walk the street. On these days I wear gold hoop earrings bought for $5.99 and rub my skin with shea butter. I never intend to go to church on a Sunday, but I make sure to wear my Sunday best, which means a modest dress that stops a couple of inches below my knees with a cardigan sweater tucked in my purse in case it gets cold. Further down the road, women and girls with short skirts and Brazilian weaves walk up and down the block waving to cars passing by. Some of them wear jeans and a T-shirt, or a dress that stops a couple inches below their knees like mine. They look like everyday people doing everyday things until a car slows down and they get in.

A friend gave unsolicited advice about my neighborhood, saying, "If you see little girls waiting on a corner, just know they're not waiting for the bus." I've got to be careful walking the street because many times I've been stopped. I try to convince myself that I'm different from the other girls on the street. I found a job at some nonprofit teaching kids from neighborhoods where the streetlights flash on and off, and there's a check-cashing store on every block. The job keeps me eating rice and beans all week but at least I'm doing some good. I think this to myself as I step out the door.

But every thought I have gets put to the test on the street, where the chill of the Bay Area sweeps up all our skirts just the same and you never know who's peeping. One man followed me for twenty minutes and finally stepped out of his car to ask if I needed a ride. I looked at him in disbelief and said, "Sir, I've reached my destination!" This isn't a walking kind of neighborhood. Not for a young woman alone. But on Sunday, after I clean, I walk. Not all people that drive slow or hang onto their street corners do that—follow people that don't want to be followed. Some call me sister, or queen, or give a nod of recognition as I walk. I never hold a glance for too long though. On this street, it's best not to linger. I've tried to walk to the end of the street, but really, it's one of the longest streets in the city.

When I walk, Ekpewan walks with me. She's the flea that won't stop buzzing in my ear. I hear her footsteps tapping beside me, and her voice leaves a tingle on the tip of my ear. She notes the trash strewn across the street, cluttered with candy wrappers, half-eaten cheeseburgers, plastic red cups, bras, and even a used tampon. We watch cars drive around potholes taking up the entire street. We pass children playing in front yards with not much room to run because everywhere is fenced in. *Why do you live here?* she asked me one time.

I snapped back at her, "Why do you follow me?" I asked this not wanting to know the answer, but she offered one anyway.

Because I don't want you picked off the street and hurt since no one will be there to care for you afterwards. And no one will want to talk about it if you do get hurt. And then you'll just become a nobody who goes nowhere. I want you to be somebody, Arit. That's my only aim here. My eyes stayed on the shifting about the street, taking in new sights I hadn't caught before.

On one walk, we happened upon a Nigerian restaurant. There, I ate fufu that reminded me of my mom's cooking, jollof rice with dodo, and a meat pie. After we had found the restaurant (and felt satisfied with the food), we started going there as part of our Sunday walks. I met a man whose voice sounded like the TV preacher I watched as a kid. He turned around to look at me while he was waiting for the cashier to ring up his meal.

"How are you?" he asked.

"Fine," I replied.

"You sound like you were born here."

"That's 'cause I was born here."

"Do you visit home often?"

"Nope."

"Why not?"

I shrugged.

Another man—I suppose his friend—turned around to join the conversation. He grabbed a greasy bag of chin-chin from the cashier while staring back at me and saying, "Are you not an adult? Why don't you go home? There's no excuse now."

"True," I answered.

"Leave her alone, brother. We all choose what we choose. Besides, it works better for me that my children don't know my language and have never visited Nigeria. They were born in Sacramento, and all they know is Sacramento. When they ask me why my accent is so funny, I tell them, this is how Black people from the South sound. And when I talk in Yoruba, they never know what I'm talking about. They don't know a damn thing, and it works better for me this way. Children asking too many questions is not a good thing."

The man with the TV-preacher voice and his friend laughed.

"My children are confused o!"

I walk to the restaurant to cry and eat. Once, a woman wearing a large hat with purple feathers caught me shedding tears while stuffing rice with red sauce down my throat. She first sat across from me, peering over her plate of rice and beans to observe me wipe my eyes and eat my meal. Finally, she picked up her plate and walked over to my table, sat herself down and asked, "Sister, why do you weep?"

I don't know what I told her, probably nothing, because in that place, people talk-talk-talk without listening, and laugh so hard that they may not hear what someone else is saying. I didn't think there was enough room for me to explain anything because she took a Bible out of her purse, recited passages from Psalms, and told me the importance of giving my life to Jesus.

"He will solve it all!" The woman stretched her rough hand to touch mine. "I tell you, you must give your life to him. Give your life to him, and you won't cry anymore, my dear."

Ekpewan weighed in. *If I were alive, I'd have given my life over to Jesus, but I don't know what he'd say about what I've seen in this country! She makes good points. If more people gave themselves over to our Dear Savior, then they would know to put their trash in the garbage. Little girls would not sell their bodies and would go to school, and the police would not be so corrupt. You wouldn't come to a restaurant to put all your business out for the world to see and cry without reason. I think I agree with this woman here. What are your thoughts on this, Arit?*

I said nothing to the woman holding my hand or to Ekpewan droning in my ear. They didn't care that I was in love with a God that looked and sounded more like me than it does them. I wiped a tear knowing that it's best not to cry on a Sunday.

The walk home is completely uphill. I'd take the bus, but I hate waiting. Sometimes I think Ekpewan works her magic to push me up the hills a little faster. I always make it to my apartment before the streetlights go on. Before I go to bed, I think about the day, and all the chores I've done to clean the tiny studio. Usually, I am satisfied with my handiwork and might watch reality TV. But this Sunday night was different. I sat up straight in bed, with the pillow wedged between my back and wall, waiting for her. My ear tingled and I knew she was near.

"Ekpewan?" I said. No sound came back, but I knew she was listening. "It's time for you to go." There was no response, but in my belly I knew she was there. She might have been squinting her eyes in discomfort, or pulling on one of my braids, whatever she was doing, I kept speaking. "I don't want to hear a word you have to say."

I stared at the floor I scrubbed, the table I disinfected with Lysol, the mirror I wiped down with white vinegar. I sat until something shifted in my belly telling me she was gone for good.

That night, I turned on pop and R&B music and added some Fela and other songs I heard in the restaurant to my growing playlist. I twirled and stomped on the floor. I looked up different spices online that I would use to make an okra soup similar to my mom's. Later that night, I drew another picture of my future self. The woman was still tall, still wearing hooped earrings, with box braids hanging past her shoulders. I drew dimples under her cheeks and gave her fire-truck-engine-red lips to add an extra punch to her picture. The fear she has known was slowly draining out of her body, that's why her knees didn't ache so much. She had sturdy legs, and she'd rather use them to walk than fly. I put the finishing touch on the woman, I drew her with her mouth open rather than closed. This time around, the woman on the paper had something to say. Under the picture I wrote, "I, Arit Essien, ask for help . . ."

I felt satisfaction at my handiwork. The woman I drew is a woman made of her own efforts. She is made from grit and elbow grease. I basked in this. Until my right hand, the hand I used to draw this woman, turned cold. My leg twitched as if it was ready to run laps or dance forever. And the twitch moving through my legs lasted through the night and the nights to follow. I never slept too well after that.

I will bind myself to her
wrestle with her
Swallow her whole
if she dare think
she can wipe me out
Unless she peels off her skin and burns her flesh
She is part of me
Her face and gait do not belong only to her
Doesn't she know I cannot help but love her?

The Girl

Nigeria, 1995. Ekpewan.

We thought her damaged. In hindsight, it was too heavy a burden for an unremarkable girl not more than eighteen, but her reputation preceded her. Her father's father was a crook chief. By crook, I mean that this man just knew how to steal. He stole from people too poor to give, and he acquired enough wealth to last his sons many decades. The land and most of the palm trees on it, he stole. I heard he was unable to see over his own stomach. Wasting his days feeding a never-ending hunger while drinking with the few men whose palms he greased. The crook went on getting more and more, while the many got less and less.

Killing him would have been easy, a drop of poison in the wine for lunch, a woman with a nice waist who'd choke him while riding him to death at night, a worthy opponent conspiring for a takeover in the dawn. Any plan, at any time, could have worked to the people's benefit. He was repulsive, leading with his protruding belly and his cock that was always at attention when a wide hip was in sight. No one could say they loved him. He was a big man with very little forethought, such an archetype in this country can easily be replaced. He continued stealing without so much as a grumble from those close to him. Not from his disgruntled house staff, or anyone tasked with putting a plate of food in his face. Despicable!

I could rationalize the plight of the poor, those faceless, overburdened people with enough woes to manage. What forethought can one have when your life is dangling from here to there on a string? My father used to say the poor can be daft when they're hungry and even dafter when they're sad. I will have to begrudgingly excuse them. But what of his unfavored wives? The men with the greased palms? Or anyone else with enough standing to overthrow the idiot? They are his co-conspirators. I tell you that for the one who wreaks monstrosity there are at least four people in the room who've allowed it.

The crook chief—privy to the fact that he was feared but not loved—threw elaborate celebrations where the feasts were plentiful. During those feasts most people forgot grievances, content to simply eat, drink, and watch the masked performance. One actor wore a mask representing the crook chief, with a big wooden stomach tied around his back. The actor played a dancing buffoon, tripping over his feet and breaking the stomach to pieces. The wooden stomach was full of all the palm trees (representing the land) and food the crook stole. Actors representing the townspeople scurried to collect the shrubs, ripped flowers, and rotten fruit falling from the broken stomach. They even took the wood back, knowing the chief stole that too.

Drunk on palm wine, the laughing people forgot their jubilation would soon end. The crook chief had won the game of wits, allowing them a measly play where they hid behind masks like mice. When the people realized they had been conned, they'd pray for the real chief to fall over his belly, possibly hitting the ground hard enough to crack his skull. Oh, but this is what weak people do! When they can't confront the source of their rage they huddle in the corner and pray for a curse. That's why the entire village believed anyone descended from the big-bellied brute was an enemy, and there was no place his offspring could go where this curse didn't follow them. News travels fast, and in this part of the world your family's reputation is like your social security number. Better make sure it checks out.

Little surprise that the girl's father was a blathering, self-centered drunkard. He squandered the money his father gave him to study abroad and marry, coming home degreeless, without his wife. Two years later, the wife, who promptly realized she could adopt the American way of doing things and divorce the fool, sent the daughter home to live with the father. The father was furious at the little girl who failed to bring her mother back. A lot to put on an infant girl, but what else is to be expected from a mother abandoning the child to study the book and a father abandoning his responsibilities for a bottle? His senior sister stepped in to raise her when the girl turned ten. She would visit the father's compound often, teaching the girl how to cook properly and supervising her daily movements. She wasn't impressed with her brother's daughter at all. Once she commented on the girl's inability to present herself as someone of exemplary capability, briefly complaining about how the girl wasn't very book smart or business-minded and could make good soup but not sweet soup.

The aunt is the only one from that family I respect. Even with all the *wahala**, I keep her in high regard. She's done well for herself. Never taking after the men in her family, she knew a pious life was best. I don't know how such an old woman found the strength to rear a child. I warned her it was too late to raise an almost-grown girl. *A child is like dough, it needs kneading and molding from the beginning. You've lost those years now.*

The old woman grunted, paying me no mind. She was a strict caretaker, confident in her ability to raise a decent girl. She spanked the child for small infractions, spanking her if she found a tiny rip in the girl's dress or if the gas was wasting long after the water had boiled. And then she spanked the child for those infractions that were beyond one's control. Like the way the child's hair grew so fast. Uncombed and coarse, it would take much work to

*Nigerian pidgin word meaning trouble

tame it, and the aunt wasn't able to spare such patience. The father had let her hair grow, ignoring that her appearance was a reflection of him, but for the aunt, a child under her roof displaying such wildness was an embarrassment of the highest order. She knew the compulsions that ruled her family line: drunks, philanderers, gluttons, spinsters, misers, thieves, and God-fearing women. But she didn't know much about the girl's mother's side, and suspected that what ran through that line was a lot of incorrigible women who could turn wild if given the chance. The aunt cut the child's hair every four days, which meant that every four days, the child got spanked.

But maybe the aunt had a point for disciplining her this way. Some years later, the girl developed thighs and breasts that poked through her Sunday school dress. A little time later she went and got herself pregnant. When people learned of the pregnancy, they shook their heads. They murmured loud enough to show disdain and spoke quietly enough to show a bit of empathy for the hard life ahead.

The aunt soon covered herself in black, lamenting that children growing up too fast was creating a generation of loose girls. In church, she gave testimony to the sadness she felt at the girl's predicament, using the story to make a case for abstinence, remarking that it was immoral for young girls to take up boyfriends in their hopes of becoming modern. The aunt became a preacher of sorts, preaching whenever she could about celibacy until marriage, using the home service she led as a way to share her renewed love of Christ, praying for no more shame to enter her household while rebuking all evil, and for the aunt, pregnancy at such a young was the very definition of evil. But I knew the truth. I was rather amazed at how she could lie, but I suppose the terrors of men make liars of us all. The real story hurt the heart.

The aunt told a handful of church women (the gossips they are) the truth. The group of women soon began spreading the word, adding their own doubts and resentments to her story, and soon everyone had heard some version of this horrendous tale because as you know, news travels fast. I was appalled at the women gossiping on a friend. That's why I curb my tongue and keep my mouth shut. These kinds of women are the first to break into tongues on the church floor, screeching that they are overcome with the anointing. Next day, they hear a bit about a woman's suffering and spread all of her business. What kind of anointing is that?

. . . *That girl's father is just as foolish as his stupid father, the crook chief, but sorry for her . . . The way some people can behave these days, even Satan himself couldn't think to do the evil the human mind can conjure . . . But she comes from a bad family o, liars all of them, and the girl may very well be a liar too, show me your people and I'll show you who you are is the adage . . . but sorry for the girl o. Sorry for her . . .*

From what she said, the girl had no choice in the matter. She was walking the red-orange road the children take to go to school. She felt a tap on her shoulder and turned around. When she turned, she saw a flying fist ready to hit her. Somewhere between falling and getting up, she remembered hearing grunts and moans and that flying fist. Judging from the embarrassment of the girl, the aunt knew the story was true.

From my own observations, I believe her story checks out. The girl was the first to memorize Psalm 23 in Sunday school. The pastor chose her to recite the psalm at the adult service. She clasped her hands in front of her dress, shouting the scripture to the entire congregation. We clapped for the girl, as we had to be polite in church. When service ended, we mumbled about why she thought it necessary to yell the Word at us. A while ago, the aunt bragged about how the girl was chosen to deliver the sacrament to her classmates. Though I scoffed at the old woman's arrogance, I'm sure her niece did her job dutifully. She appeared to be a dutiful girl.

The gossips said the aunt scoured the market, the church, the school, and the red-orange road searching for a flying fist. A bruise. A scratch. A welt. A clue. She examined the hands of any man or boy she caught in those places. Goodness, can you imagine? A woman of her station brought down to finding a wound on a fist? A pity.

The girl's stomach got bigger, and no one could stop gossiping about the motherless child giving birth to a fatherless child. Every day there was news about the girl. Some gossip I knew was true. Most of the information was rubbish. One bit of truth concerned the father. If the baby was a boy, the father said he'd raise him. If the baby was a girl, then he'd travel to bless the newborn and move on with his day. She became the aunt's house girl, a further punishment for her condition. I couldn't blame the aunt for taking this position, if it weren't for her Christian hospitality the girl might have been on the street.

They went to church every Sunday, and the girl read to the pupils for children's service. From the looks of her, she appeared to be faring well. At least that's what the aunt claimed after she died. But permit me to tell a bit of what happened to her, a bit of what I saw with my own two eyes and heard with my own two ears. And let me be clear that we are of no relation and other than the occasional greeting I would have no reason to speak with her. But I am compelled to speak on her behalf as I'm certain I'm the closest to this girl's truth simply because I care enough to talk about what I saw that day.

A trail of blood led to that red-orange road. Crows and stray cats were pecking a carcass in the distance. The girl's insides, mainly her guts, led to her body, which no one could call a body after the animals had feasted. A crowd formed in disbelief, calling the terrible sight wicked. That evening, the church held an emergency service because as you know, news travels fast. The pastor spoke fervently about death and wayward girls. The congregation whispered in the pews. Some speculated, wondering if the flying fist killed her; others stated she had taken her own life. No one walked that road for three months. Not a child, not an adult, not a cow, not me.

Let's go back to when I was fifteen, it was a nice age. I was bright in the face and fatter, but fatter because I was eating well, not fatter because I was eating for two. I was a girl who had dreamt of painting her nails in glitter and straightening her hair once it grew back. I was busy thinking of how to work out the lisps in my mouth to talk smoothly, the way I'd heard real Americans talk. I liked to stand in front of the mirror learning to talk without any clicks, ticks, or sing-songy notes coming from my voice. Americans mumble and speak bland. I needed to learn how to mumble and speak bland too, because soon I'd see my mum, and I needed to make a good impression. I had a good plan that I was keeping to myself, no one but God knew about it and it was a fine plan: Meet Mum in the land of jeans and T-shirts. Go to school there. But before I could go there I had to turn things around and get my marks up so I could get into a good university close to her, and I knew the perfect school: Harvard. I thought of what I would write when I told her I was coming.

Dear Mum,

How are you? I'm doing very well. I've been accepted into such-and-such university. Will you pick me up from the airport? I miss you.

Sincerely,

Your Daughter

I dreamt of wearing faded jeans when boarding the plane. I wanted to travel in style, like a real American girl. I remember giggling to myself, thinking about the letters she would write.

My Dear Daughter,

Congratulations! I've missed you too. Such-and-such university is only an hour away from me. I insist that you let me drive you to your classes. No daughter of mine will stay in campus dorms. You must stay with me because now we can make up for lost time. To make it up to you, I'll take you to get your first cheeseburger—it's best when you eat it with lots of ketchup and yellow cheese. Well done.

Yours,

Mum

The pastor had spoken that year about how one could do all things through Christ. I had obviously read that passage before, but he also mentioned something interesting that made me look at that scripture in a new way. He said: "Glory be to God when you're finally victorious." He pointed to the congregation while wiping his brow and asked: "Who's a winner out there?" And there was no other option but to say: "Me", because no one would want to be a loser. Aunty called him a con man that was getting people too excited when the service ended. "Does he not see how the opportunities are dwindling in this country? Kai!" She said, "If they want to win, they better find someone who can get them a job." But there was no other option than to listen to the pastor and take his word as fact. He spoke like he believed in us, like he wasn't trying to talk us down. After hearing him speak, I decided that by senior year, I would graduate with top marks in my class and have the pick of any university I wanted. My classmates liked to show off about attending a school in London, Canada, or France. I never bragged about where I wanted to go, even though back then I believed I was going to do better than all of them. I'd smile when thinking of how I'd stand before my classmates while the teacher praised how I was the only one going to America. I would tell my teacher of my acceptance after I found out where everyone else was going. By then, it would be too late for anyone to change their minds. I know it's not good to keep secrets or wish bad things on your mates, but I wanted my plan to come true. I'd turn into a smooth-talking American girl with good marks to impress my mother. A good smart girl—with good fashion—but not so worldly that I'd cause her worry. When the day came to board the plane I'd forget everything. And when Mummy saw me, she'd forget everything too. I'd tell her not to worry herself, that all was well and that it was better we forget. The only thing was to leave and leave fast.

Actually, the day it happened, I was caught daydreaming about going abroad. It was a sweet thing to think about since my marks had never gotten very high, but I took it easy on myself a bit, because I had studied hard, I had tried. The dream was so real that when I'd felt that tap on my shoulder, I was certain it was my mother . . . but I think someone had found out about my hope. Someone must have heard and got worried that I'd find a way to go abroad. People can plot to destroy you if they see you hoping for something more. There's a lot of that going around now. People blocking you because they're jealous. I only told God what I wanted and it's possible that Jesus heard my secret too, since whenever I end a prayer I say, "In Jesus Christ's Name." I also told the picture of my mother hidden under my pillow. I thought they were the only ones who knew, but Aunty says that people can see when you are getting too excited. Maybe in all my prayers and daydreams, someone was seeing too much joy from me. They were most likely wondering what I was hiding and became angry when they saw that I was acting too free.

At first I thought the blood was my menses. I asked God to make the blood *be* my menses, but the next day the blood left, and I knew I better be scared. I kept praying for an answer, but before an answer could come Aunty found out somehow. Maybe someone also told her what happened, it's possible. She came with a fallen tree branch ready to beat me. *A girl sneaking around to vomit and hide her stomach is a girl taking lovers in the dark. Who have you cheapened yourself for? Good girls don't behave like harlots.*

I told her all I had was the memory of a fist and strange noises, of waking up on the road with dirt on my knees and blood in my underwear. It may have been smarter to have said nothing because she kept beating me, over and over, until I heard myself cry out. Somewhere in between my pleas, she stopped to listen. I don't think she really believed me, because after the beating she went to tell everyone I wasn't a good girl. She said I should be grateful because God was merciful and forgave loose girls if they walked the right path, but she said my life would be hard.

I prayed in the morning, after school, and at night. I prayed in between sweeping the floors and washing the pots. I prayed for God to get me to the end of my pain, so I could pick up where I left off in my dream. It was a good one to keep coping until I found a new plan, but it was hard to think about it without thinking of falling to the ground. I had been okay with knowing I wouldn't get into a prestigious school to get me closer to her, but I could have found another way to follow her there and not have this all be so disappointing. I could have managed that. I wanted the strength to get past the flying fist, past the baby in my tummy, and past the birth. I'd be a little plumper from the baby, but once I left, no one would guess what happened. I would keep that to myself and move on.

I prayed for forgiveness, for keeping secrets, for being bad, and for daydreaming too much. I also prayed for the baby to be a boy because if it was a girl, I'd have to take care of it and live with Aunty. I asked God to forgive me for being selfish and demanding a boy, but I couldn't help it. The plane, the cheeseburger, the glitter nails, the smooth-talking English, the long hair, the chance to be an American girl, pretty and without a scratch—I didn't want to give these things up. I got afraid that God wasn't listening when I couldn't see my dream anymore and couldn't imagine a new one. When I dreamt of boarding the plane, I heard a crying baby. A baby girl would crawl to me, crying in a way that let me know I couldn't board the plane. I wasn't happy to dream anymore, and I knew He had read between the lines too.

I knew the baby was going to be a girl the day I heard crying in my tummy. Every day the baby cried. It sounded awful, like someone trying to scream through a bottle. When I recited my prayers, she would cry. If I daydreamed about writing letters to my mother, she would cry. If I tried to choose a boy's name for her, she would cry. When she cried it felt like my belly was shaking. If she didn't cry, then she'd kick, and the way she kicked was not like the kicks I expected. Aunty told me that babies tug at the tummy if they need food or to remind their Mums they're ready to live their earthly lives. But I think the baby kicked because she knew I could never love her. If it came out a boy, I would leave the first chance I got; if it came out a girl, I would hate her because she'd put me under pressure. Aunty made me drink a special tonic when I complained of pain, but nothing was helping. She took me to the doctor when I couldn't take the crying and kicking anymore. The doctor said I was fine. Aunty said she didn't want to hear any more of my complaints even if they were true. "Every woman has pain," she said, "and you're a woman now."

My last night here was painful. I thought I was going into labor because it felt like my insides were whirling. I screamed, hoping Aunty would hear me, but she never came. I hummed to the baby, trying to quiet her down. The kicks were like jagged stones cutting my insides, and finally, her kicks ripped me open. The baby jumped out, pulling me along a slimy rope, spilling blood and intestines on the floor.

I checked between her legs, doing this because it would have been nice to see a hanging piece of skin, it would have been okay if she were a boy, I could cope. But a girl, hey! A girl. For what? Her small face could fit into my hand, my hand could press into her nose and mouth, and her breathing could end, this would be very okay. I wouldn't mind this, but then I'd have to see the hands I used to suffocate her every day and that is too disturbing. I would also have to explain how she died, and that's all I've been doing since this baby came, explaining that this isn't my fault, explaining that I didn't choose this, and it's a problem when your life becomes a sad explanation. I can't tell you how discouraged I felt. But if I could let myself do this, cover her small face with my palm, press my palm into her nose and mouth, and have this done, it would be okay. Very okay. I don't like doing bad things, but I wanted life to stop frustrating me at every turn. I'm not a bad girl. I promise.

It was too late to tell the baby to not flee. I had lost all rights of a mother, and she looked happy to be away from me. I tried holding her, but she screamed when I went to grab her. I pleaded so much that I began to lie. If soothing words couldn't help, maybe a lie could. I said many lies that night. Too many to count. I promised that I would dream a dream of the two of us. I told her I would take her on the plane, feed her my favorite foods, and tell my mother about her. I lied, and she screamed, knowing that I was nothing but a liar.

She ran, ripping the rope out of me, and all I could do was run after her. I stumbled on rock, slime, and grass, running through a night of jet black and tears. Ran until my feet gave out, until smooth breathing became rough, until running turned to sleeping.

But then everyone has to open their eyes to see another life if they walk away from an old one. There's no end. That's the first thing I learned lying there with blood leaking out. So imagine that a thought can move quickly in this new place. You think about it and it appears. Seeing this happen was frightening at first, but that's the standard in this world. Had I known I could simply think myself into being, perhaps my human life wouldn't have been so difficult. But that's the human world for you. Humans are the builders. Their lives are paid for in toil. Everything about humans takes effort. But I'm in a place where there's no need for that kind of labor, praise God. I met my Guide the night I died because I had simply thought of her. I didn't know her, but all the strain made me immediately wish for her, and so she arrived.

"Wake up," she ordered.

I guessed that she had a sagging face, a straight full mouth, and eyes that had developed a film over them, causing her brown eyes to turn gray. I guessed that I'd have to call her Aunty or Mummy, a name to show she had more years of life than I did. The sound of her voice proved me right, as it sounded tattered around the edges and not very gentle.

"Follow me," she said.

When I looked up, there was a floating human above me.

"I can't," I replied.

"You can." She was sure I could do it. "Turn yourself into a bird, any bird, and follow me. You must take this particular form to get up. Don't you want to get up?"

I could barely stand on my two feet as a human and now she wanted me to fly.

"Why waste yourself this way? You would have told someone you were suffering, nau. Someone could have doused you with the anointing. Slapped you with the holy ghost, pushed a revival down your throat to keep you alive. If you needed relief there were herbs to chew, advisors to consult. Why disgrace yourself this way? You're lucky you can move on to the next thing. All is well. But your earthly life is finished and your child is dead. So fly, nau."

I would have stayed in the dirt to avoid having to hear her go on and on. If the next life meant another round of always saying yes Aunty and lowering my head it probably was better to let a bird peck my flesh than actually turn into one. But then the night was very cool, and my body could not stop shaking.

"I'm going. You better follow," she announced.

I shut my eyes on the woman floating above me. If I was some place between life and the unknown then maybe it was possible to form claws and wings. My mouth watered, soaking up the dryness in my mouth while I sloshed a coppery taste around. She was moving further away into the darkness. So then I gulped down my spit, said a quick prayer, and went after her.

To the Children Growing Up
in the Aftermath of Their Parents' War
Massachusetts, late 1990s. Arit.

All of us are scoundrels. The soldier, the general, the president, the first lady, the farmer, the architect, the husband, the wife, the pastor, the nun, the witch doctor, the westerner, the native, the butcher, the bushman, the city dweller, the brother, the daughter, the son, the father, the mother, the aunt, the uncle, the old, the young, the saint, the sinner, the virgin, the whore—down to the girl-child digging in the dirt to plant a seed. That's what I gather from surviving the touch of war. The first thing a war does is dislocate skin from bone, head from neck, and joint from finger until it moves to dislocating nations, lands, and regions.

I surmise that when the war touched my parents, something in their biochemistry mutated and poisoned them with a bit of scoundrel.

The infection was meant to stay for the purpose of surviving the unthinkable, like beholding decapitated limbs and rearranged faces that showed the handiwork of war on a body. Inch by inch the infection took over their sense of goodness. Take my mother's story about the war she survived. The war that displaced her heart. She was seven years old when it happened.

"I don't want it to touch me ever again. No thank you!"

That was her declaration to the civil war she survived. The war of 1967. Her father had moved everyone to live with their grandmother where the gunshots wouldn't follow them.

"It didn't matter if you were Igbo or not. If somebody holds a gun to your head, you have to pick a side. These soldiers could gouge your eyes out, chop your limbs, and plunge the butt of their guns into your heart, because in war, that's the last thing you should have. A heart."

My mother told me that as soon as she returned home from the war she went out to the garden. Digging in the dirt and planting seeds were her favorite things to do. But when she dug into the earth, she found a human skull. The skull had a gash above its right eye with worms and insects scattering about. She took the skull to her mother and her mother grabbed the skull and threw it in the bush. Later that day, the girl-child (that's my mother) and her siblings found the skull and decided to kick around the decapitated head as if it were a soccer ball. When it was my mother's turn to kick the skull, it shattered to pieces. She never told me if she got to plant the seeds that day, but this story let me know the war infected her with a dose of scoundrel.

I imagine my mother's heart had emptied into the toilet after the skull broke. Her heart must have known there wouldn't be much use for it in a world like hers. It's easier to imagine my mother pooping out her heart than imagining her as a child who liked to play for the hell of it. It's difficult to see her chasing butterflies or stomping ants for sport. She never smiles because the lines around her lips keep her face hanging down. And that's what the scoundrel wants from its victims. No heart, no whimsy. Joy is its kryptonite. It's always looking for its next high. On the prowl.

That's where my generation comes in. The generation of iPhones, text messages, and soundbites. The generation of instant gratification and American arrogance. The generation once removed from their parents' homeland. We wager that if we're born in the land of milk and honey, we'll never starve to the point of our stomachs blowing up like balloons or stumble upon gashed skulls. We expect our parents to come into our present moment, the world of skyscrapers and TV you can stream, IMAX, and all-you-can-eat Chinese buffets, tankinis, and dreams of wearing tons of sequins because you're famous (or because you've won the lottery).

We're scoundrels too. Well, scoundrels-in-training. We've been infected with the need to prove ourselves while carrying our parents' grief. We don't account for our parents' devastation, and we couldn't care less about their sadness until it hurts us. We don't know what to make of the fact that we're our parents' creation and their devastation. They love us, but they can't stand us because we're so removed from what they know. Our generation is primed to pass on contempt for where we come from to the next generation if we're not careful. That's another casualty we inherit from the war our parents survived.

There is *one* way to break the cycle of scoundrelism. When it infects you, it'll ask one question: *Are you gonna tell what happened?* You'll hear the question in your sleep or in those moments when there's too much space between your next thought and action. It's up to you to answer yes or no. If you do tell a story about what happened to you, you'll start to feel lighter. When you share a lesson you've learned with someone who wants to hear your story, the scoundrel begins to shrink. Some days your story will hurt so much it makes you cry, and other days your story hurts so much it makes you laugh. But all that matters is the infection loses its hold on you.

Most people choose to trap their stories inside of them, thinking it's easier to live with the devil they know rather than facing the devil they don't. I don't think my parents have shared their stories because when I'm around them I can feel that something's weighing them down. My mother tells me that one story of when the war first touched her almost like we're in a confessional. My father admits absolutely nothing, which lets me know that when the scoundrel asked him the question, he said no. I've heard some of my "uncles" and "auntys" mention the war in passing. They mention it while eating or just before getting ready to laugh. They won't call it a war or lament too long about it. They'll just take a moment to pause and say, *remember*, and then follow up with a quick, "It must not happen again!"

I call them "uncles" and "auntys" because they're not my real blood relatives. They visited us from time to time and I have fond memories of them. They used to pinch my cheeks, kiss my forehead, and give me all the Reese's Pieces I wanted. My dad says they immigrated here with one portmanteau and barely any money in their pockets. So I guess we're family because our migration stories are more or less the same.

We're Ibibio and I heard somewhere that Ibibio means brief. Even our talk of war is just a mere pause in the cluster of tasks we must get through in the day. As a child, I always caught their pauses, probably because I knew their silence had little to do with my understanding but everything to do with theirs. I often asked my mother about my father. What happened to him? I needed to know why his particular brand of scoundrel made him so fragmented and violent. Couldn't he just take after my mother and become tired and sad?

My mother told me that his brother had left to fight with a gun in his hand and returned with that same gun latched over his shoulder and half his face blown off. I suppose if I saw my brother maimed, something in my mind might unhinge too. But that's the thing about our generation. We live in the aftermath of our parents' war, and we're the ones who have to deal with the scoundrel they can't release. So in a way, their war has touched us too.

How did I survive my parents' war? Joy. It was my penchant and almost hedonistic tendency to be happy. I'm not talking about a happiness dependent on finding a man, having kids, a great career, nice clothes, and people who know your name. I'm not even talking about the happiness that requires food on the table. That's what I call the checklist happiness, the happiness where you mark a check next to each item as if it's a to-do list. That sort of happiness doesn't last long because there's always more to put on the list. Before you know it, you're obsessed with checking off items and overwhelmed with all the accumulated stuff you have to take care of.

I'm talking about a just-because sort of happiness. Like the unapologetic joy of drag queens when they decide it's a damn good day to dress the world in glitter. Like the glee of a child wearing a cape and pretending they can fly. Like the spontaneous combustion of a brass band playing in the middle of the street and stopping traffic. Like belly laughing when everyone is bent on being serious. Like wiping your tears when you get slapped and smiling to yourself because you know your story doesn't end with someone else's brutality. It's the possibility of streaking the world in something different, if even for a moment.

I did everything I could do for just-because happiness. I took a bedsheet and wore it as a cape to pretend I was a bird. I stomped my feet and shook my ass because I was taken with the rhythm of my own dancing. I joined the show choir to sing my heart out even though I knew I'd catch hell for the racy uniform when I got home. In a house bent on suffering, I pressed the joy button. My natural inclinations infuriated and bewildered my parents. I sought out just-because happiness at all costs. Even if that meant letting go of what my parents believed. It was that wild child calling in joy that kept me going until I was safe enough to tell my story. My wild child felt that at any moment she could paint the world the color of a rainbow and call it a day. Sometimes I still believe that I can color the world if I find big enough crayons. But I've got a lot to deal with. I have a wild child that wants to be free, a scoundrel wanting to spread its poison, and my parents saying I better honor my roots.

Ekom and I were tasked with taking the trash out. That's my sister's name, Ekom. Anyone with that name has to be round in the face and funny on Tuesdays or else they shouldn't be named Ekom. Okon—our brother with the Tyrannosaurus rex T-shirt as his permanent attire—was probably across my room asleep. I believe so anyway, as I do think I heard snoring that day and I assure you if there was snoring then the noise absolutely led to the room where he rested. Anyone with the name Okon must wear the exact T-rex shirt he does or else how can I really say they're an Okon? And then how could I say that I'm an Arit if there is more than one of my brother and sister in another place?

No other Okons, Ekoms, or Arits exist in these woods, where the roads wind and the baby deer cross the street, and the garbage truck treks up the hill with two burly men in navy green jumpsuits hopping off the trunk to heap trash into the truck. And we know these garbage collection men because they are here every Thursday morning to give us a wave if they see us riding our bikes (Okon on his trike) in the front yard. They do not know any other Okons, Ekoms, or Arits living in the woods, and they find our names odd, but I assure you that their names are quite basic and because of how basic their Wonder Bread names are, I always assume one of them is probably named Todd.

Our plan was to finish our chores so we could watch a rerun of our favorite show—*A Different World*—consuming Kimberly, Whitley, Jaleesa, Dwayne Wade, Winnie, and Walter, all to say, *gunna be me soon, yup, gunna be me.* What other metropolitan world to consume while we ached to spit out the grass and dirt choking us while we stayed stuck in the middle of a forest. The city meant Whitley high heels and cherry-colored lipstick, not dollar store flip flops with a stained T-shirt.

My father marched upstairs a second after Kim's first appearance on the show. She barged into the scene huffing in distress, making me conclude that strong women wore MC Hammer pants and opened doors making a witty statement. Ekom clapped showing her affinity for Kim's bold move and I meekly tsked at my incapability of bombastic entrances and a dearth of wit.

My father looked out the window. "Do you not see this, here?" He jabbed an index finger towards the street. The crows had pecked apart the trash bags, leaving everything floating down the hill. "Why have you let this happen? You should have double-bagged the bags." He blamed us for the crows that pecked the trash, the trash floating down the hill, and for the fact that the neighbors would see that the only children in the woods named Okon, Ekom, and Arit couldn't keep their garbage in the bag.

A moment later he vanished downstairs. As Whitley sauntered onto the screen, my father marched upstairs clutching a stick. The stick came from wooden hangers we used to hang church clothes on. The perfect weapon if you wriggle the rod from the wooden hanger.

My teeth pressed together as Whitley's nasally voice disappeared into the background. Ekom could have turned down the volume, but I can't confirm this. My center of gravity was rapidly flushing out of my system and the only lucid thoughts I had were three. The first thought was of my dry hands. Oil on the hands, jojoba, canola, or olive would relieve the spanking a tinge, creating a buffer. Mom was gone to work, a forty-five-minute drive away. Not one of us could sneak away to say, "He didn't come up singing, he came up in a rage. Help us, please." Number two. If she were here, my mother, she'd be sleeping, and I think she did this because her family had enough money to hide during the war. They ate snails that washed up on the shore and wild mushrooms but mostly she gained a penchant for napping through disaster, and why think of this story anyway when your mother has gone to work? Thinking of her sleeping is a more comforting thought than whatever will transpire in this parlor, with the volume down, and his voice so shrill, and a part of me imagining I am walking out the door, drifting down the hill with the trash. The stick hit the hollow center of my palm and I careened back to lucid thought number one. My hands were dry, and I could see the splotchy red mark that every thwap left. A thrash on the edge of your finger could make you yelp in two minutes, and a thrash on the tender place under your pinky could make you wail on sight. Ekom's hands were hit too, but were hers mine and mine hers? I can't confirm this. Then his ranting, my father spouting his demands, "Go outside and pick up that trash. We didn't come here to be embarrassed."

This brings me to thought number three. My father had no money to flee the gunshots, so he became war itself. Unleashing attacks on targets and stacking bodies around him, I was convinced he stored them in the basement closet, and it was the ghosts of these bodies that spooked him into beating down the living.

Ekom, the sister with more clout in the household, tried reasoning over the shouting and thwapping. "Daddy, please, it's the crows . . ." She mopped the floors, washed the dishes, called the doctor, and got us to bed, and mimicked Mom's authority in her absence. But oh how this went wrong! A child telling a grown man what to do? Thwap, thwap thwap! Our palms reddened into a lashed splotch.

If only we could make the crows leave the trash alone and stop the wind from blowing the trash down the street! But if the crows still pecked the trash, and the trash still blew down the street, then what would we do about the watchful neighbors shaking their heads at our inability to contain our trash?

"Go double-bag the trash, now," he ordered.

We picked up the soggy garbage. Double-bagged the bags. Then, after sulking and sniffling seemed useless, we increased the volume to watch *A Different World*. Soon as Dwayne Wade appeared in goofy glasses with his megawatt smile, our father appeared. Ekom lowered the volume. The crows had feasted again without our catching them. They had the upper hand with their pointy beaks. No amount of pleading helped. We'd have to stay outside and fight these birds. And maybe the wind was pestering us too, because the wind had skirted the trash down the street, so maybe it was time to fight the wind too. Thwap-thwap-thwap. He'd spank us until the garbage collector arrived, that's what he said, "I'll spank you until these collectors get here."

Maybe we could have asked our watchful neighbors to look the other way if they saw floating trash and prayed they wouldn't spot the tremor in our voices. As the only Okons, Ekoms, and Arits on the street, could we afford to trust the neighbors with our red hands?

We quadruple-bagged the trash and had a stakeout watching for crows. Thirty minutes passed and we didn't see any creatures looking to ambush the garbage. We felt a bit of relief, believing we had won over the crows. I went to the bathroom while my sister made herself a bologna sandwich. We giggled and made jokes while watching a superhero cartoon. An hour must have passed before he came upstairs to look out the window. A feeling of desperation zipped through me. Thwap-thwap-thwap.

What happened next is a blur, that's the thing about surviving a war, you can blackout. Okon soon woke up, and Dad soon went downstairs, and we were left with each other for a few minutes in a corner beyond the earshot of our brother increasing the volume on a superhero cartoon.

"I'm angry," she said.

"Me too." I nodded.

"We got to tell Mom."

"She's stressed."

"He's rip shit."

"It's not so bad."

"I hate him."

"Mom's dealt with this for twenty years. Does *she* hate?"

"But we're not her."

"But I'm the first. Try being the first. You wouldn't be able to hack it."

The Birth

Nigeria and the United States,
mid-to-late 1970s, post-Biafran War. Uduak.

They told her time is a thing that runs and you must catch it. Save the leaf from autumn, freeze the snow from winter, grab the blossom from spring, and store the heat from summer. *Ini mme ọtọ ibette owo.* You better catch what you can. She was ready to leave, packing light on traditional clothing and memory. It was an exciting time and she had opted to wear jeans with her hair plaited in two tight braids for the ride. Hair pulled so tight there was no room for a single coil to breathe its way out. That's how she liked it, despite people making snide remarks, wondering why she chose to wear the hairstyle of a girl when everyone was getting their coils pressed. In her mind, she wasn't much older than a small girl. Her schooling away from home had made her more refined perhaps, but a girl nonetheless. Nineteen. Breasts the size of apples, a tiny hump for a backside, and a voice that never went above a peep. She didn't fill out the school uniform like her classmates, having grown vertically but not very much sideways like the other girls. And with development comes practice, of which she had had none. She didn't consider herself a pro at much, but she excelled at doing the right thing. And the right thing would forever be: Fulfilling whatever mandate had come from the top. Whether it had come from God, her parents, an elder, or a chairman, these beings were always in the right, and by some chance, if they weren't, it was her duty to blot out their transgressions and quietly forgive their blunders. Forgiving them erased any wrongdoing because it was evident they'd never say sorry. She had accepted that nineteen was an age of fulfilling expectations, where the ones with authority draped you in their aspirations and then paraded you out to tell the public who you are. That's how she had rationalized her arranged marriage. It was a day where she would show up and become whoever she was told to be.

The title of wife had been given to her in a wedding that she didn't have to organize. Pans of food were laid out across tables, filling an entire room for two hundred guests. One hundred of those names were invited and the other hundred names were of those who attended because they knew they wouldn't get thrown out. It would be horrible for someone to call them cheap, saying something like: Look at how stingy you are, taking your wedding to your state so that no one will come eat your rice.

Those who planned the wedding were adamant that the invited and uninvited would eat well.

There were flashing lights from cameras that clicked well into the night. She wore a white dress with a veil touching her ankles. Her hair was pressed until it was limp across her neck, which had brought tears to her mother's eyes. The young bride was required to look the part of a woman, and on that day she finally fit the bill, though she wouldn't smile in her photos for fear of her gap tooth showing. The cameraman gave her directions. Chin up. Shift head to the right. Show your teeth. That sort of thing. When the nineteen-year-old refused to follow the last demand, her mother grew alarmed. "All the women from my side have a hole between their teeth," she said. "It's the best thing about us, you know."

Then came the pictures she took with the man who had been given the title of husband. The man she often saw in church and at family gatherings. The man whose father had a cushy government job where he sent his subordinates to a Lebanese restaurant to buy him chicken shawarma (a delight their wages could not afford) while he was on a call with his minister friend who controlled the movement of oil in the Delta. Her soon-to-be husband would send for her after settling himself in Texas. They would begin university in the fall.

All this was told to her over akara and pap. Her favorite breakfast. When the house help—Taye—placed the tray in front of her, she knew it wasn't because her Mum simply wanted her to have an enjoyable meal. "Look," her mother said, while she chewed the bean cake. "You'll send some akara to Dr. Nyong's son. You know he likes to eat this too? And since you'll have to do these things for your husband one day, no better time than to start now." The bean cake didn't taste as sweet after her mother spoke. Dr. Nyong had four sons but after a few bites she realized which son she'd be delivering her beloved fritters to. What a waste, she lamented, still trying to savor the taste. Sad the way you can lose your taste for a thing with the mention of a name. That was the day she learned she'd marry Usen. He was the son who still needed a marriage.

What she knew of him was that he was a few years her senior and demanded that everyone who was not his elder call him Samuel. When he whined for his Christian name, she wanted to say, you a Samuel? Na wa. It was no good that name. And anyone with sense could see that.

Before, she'd been content to give him a quick greeting and pass on to a more pleasing personality, but now that her sights had rested on him, she couldn't help but notice the worst. He had a terrible habit of lowering his eyes in the presence of whoever he believed held more power than him, not in a sheepish or endearing way, but in a way that suggested he was sure they would see him for what he was. In the presence of her father and mother he'd prostrate himself, letting the sweaty bald spot in the middle of his head become the focal point of familiarity. He was always cowering which made him puny, not the cowering itself, but the fact that whatever he was cowering for was purely out of habit.

On a day when they were left alone, they walked through the garden in her compound, remaining quiet for the first leg of the stroll until he broke his silence. "I can take eba with a good edikaikon soup," he said. "Pounded yam is okay, too. You'll learn what I like." Out of view from their parents and staff, she saw exactly who he was. And she'd have to forgive all his errors because next to God, her parents, and her elders, he'd soon be given the title of husband and her nineteen-year-old life would be his.

Everything she could carry was put in one portmanteau, made of mottled brown leather with a thick black strap wrapped around the middle, fastened with a buckle. She had packed precisely, folding the clothes to one side. *You're supposed to lay them down flat to make more room.* That's a trick her mother taught her while fussing that she must keep that head of hers in the books, come back more intelligent than she had left, and start a proper family with her husband.

"Why the long face, dear?" her mother asked.

The daughter's eyebrows had burrowed deeper into her face, causing her eyes to blink as if they caught dust.

"I'm seeing how to fit in the shoes," she replied.

"Well, call Taye if you can't do it. Better enjoy the help for a bit before you go to run your own household."

"Hmm."

"What is it? You're looking dull." The mother held her daughter by the chin. "You'll return when school finishes," she offered. "Have your babies over there if you must, but raise them here. That's what all this is about anyway, it's about grabbing what you can from there and having a life. That's what we're after, okay?" Her mother placed a pair of shoes at the bottom of the suitcase, taking out the clothes and starting again. *Shoes go at the bottom first, then put the clothes on top, like this. You'll have to know these things for yourself, dear. Time to be focused now.*

It was easier for her mother to organize a suitcase than to waste time explaining the reason behind her stance to send her away to another land. Besides, the daughter already knew what the mother would say. If a marriage could help the family's financial constraints then what else could be done? So long as the man cared for her—cared not loved—then what more? Maybe love would come when they got older, but it wasn't a prerequisite for a long-lasting union. A life must move forward, and marriage speeds up the process, which will allow the rest of it to follow. And you—a small girl who's all of nineteen—will learn. Girls on the cusp of becoming women always learn. And I had to become a woman way before you, so what grounds are there for a quarrel?

She instructed her daughter to pack less—*you'll bring more home, trust me. Coats, toys, perfumes, chocolates, jeans, shoes, electronics, a degree, awards—don't come home empty-handed, understand?* The prestige of studying outside was the real prize but coming back with a suitcase full of gifts was a good way to decorate one's success. There was no doubt she had achieved an accomplishment, and so, she was given many blessings.

Go well. Hold on to God. Pray.

But then there was another voice that added dread to the well wishes. It maddened the nineteen-year-old how one note of discord could set everything adrift. She had fought with this voice before, the voice that belonged to the spindly woman who—as God would have it—was her grandma. How her mother, the elegant ostrich-like figure she was, came from such a gruff creature was baffling. Her mother had soft hands and a kind tone that showed she hadn't been too rough on herself. Her mother's hair—like hers—was thin. A light rub of oil or cream on a strand and a comb could easily slide through. But her grandma's hair was too thick. Long and tightly coiled. Streaked with black as most of her hair was gray bordering on white. Plenty of combs had cracked on their way down her mane. There wasn't an ounce of pleasantness to be found anywhere in the old woman. Her voice sounded like it had been skirted across a gravel road, and her hands were disturbingly humongous and veiny, with dirt under the nails. The unusual enormity of her hands made little sense, but it seemed to fit because she was always kneeling to pick out the weeds in the garden.

"Don't ask me why she still farms," her mother would say in exasperation. "We have money now and she's smart. Very smart. I can't tell you how she got so smart though. But she's sharp…just leave her."

The grandma told those who balked in disapproval to watch her bum bum while she bent over the plants to work. Uncouth. That's what the nineteen-year-old girl's father called the old woman, and he was well within his rights to call her whatever he liked in his household. That's what her mother called her in a backroom out of earshot, of course, and that's what the children and house staff thought but would never utter.

The plaited-haired girl never liked her, possibly because she couldn't comprehend her, but more because the old woman had chosen to be defiant in the midst of a well-provided-for life. The mother had married wisely, by some amazing feat, and her union had pulled the old woman out of the village and into a stately house in the city. They could eat bread with butter while enjoying the comforts of their soups and stews. They'd have their Nigerian pidgin, their native tongue, and speak the proper British English when need be. It was the price of progress, renouncing the old ways for the new while putting one foot in front of the other, but her grandma made it seem like she would never truly fit in the world that her mother had chosen for them.

The rest of the family made do with the grandma's rattling, but for some reason the girl couldn't forgive what she perceived as a willful backwardness. The grandma sensed her repulsion and soon began the dance of oil and water. She always caught the girl behaving out of character, and it was this weakness of the girl's that became her leverage. Like the time the girl stomped on the garden in a fit, destroying everything in sight. It was her aim to flatten the plants beneath her feet and grind them back into the dirt. She had a thirst to destroy something that day and wouldn't have dared to break the fine china sitting in her father's house. So she went outside and ripped what she could. Disfiguring a plant was much better than finding a decapitated finger or a bone belonging to a body. But then two hands crumpled like used paper bags grabbed her by the waist. Such worn hands should never be able to win a fight, let alone restrain whip-smart school-aged girls, but they did. The grip was so tight that her legs couldn't wriggle away.

"You are wicked!" Grandma cried. "Don't you know they will bury me here, among the flowers?" She chased the girl, and in her haste, tripped over a plastic bucket. Anyone would have spotted the bucket, but since she was losing her sight she had missed it. With every year her sight got worse and when she was riled up she'd bump into chairs and objects that she couldn't see. But she didn't let her impairment keep her from the job at hand. She saw her target, crossing to and fro in the daylight and soon caught her, flaying the girl's behind as the appetizer to the disturbance she'd cause at dinner. The little girl didn't know it, but she had given Grandma what she needed to push certain members of the family to do what she wanted. And she was jumping at the chance to terrify them. "See," she said, chewing kpomo at the table. "Una no raise a good girl at all. She do, yes ma, yes sir, to you, but to me, she dey come waste my flowers. All my hard work for my burial ground, finish. You have fine house and fine things but the girl no dey try." This could have been said for all the grandchildren at the table, as each child in one way or another had their crueler points, but the old woman spent that evening arguing for the soul of her daughter's fourth child.

It was decided that perhaps light farm work could build good character in the girl. It might not soften the heart, but it could bring humility. She was to garden with the grandmother every Saturday, and this is how the girl became privy to the thoughts and inclinations of the old woman. The girl wondered how it was possible for her to plant flowers if she couldn't see. It was bizarre, but she figured the woman was half witch anyway, another fact that frightened her and her mother, although her mother never mentioned a word about this. But all daughters know what their mothers hide on some level, and she knew that her mother's repulsion was because Grandma was the very definition of bedlam. But spending Saturdays with a woman that pressed her hands into the dirt while saying, "Well done," made it possible to not discount her entirely.

Now that it was time for her to leave, she felt caught by the old woman again.

"Keep yourself well, you hear?" she said. "Remember that your husband is no good, but since we know this is a fact and you have married you'll find a way. That country will take too much from you and then your stupid husband will collect his own piece, but don't let them take your name. That is your own."

Ooh-dwak. Uduak.

"Go well," Grandma said. "The wisdom I give is not so bad o, you can hear what people can't hear, and see what people can't see. Fine gifts for a fine girl."

Nobody knew Uduak was ready to let herself lie there that day. She had woken up with that feeling. It was a feeling sitting in the pit of her stomach with no thought of leaving. Her eyes cracked open a bit, enough to see the wrinkles in the bedding where a body should have been. She pulled the covers towards herself and turned away from where the bed was cold.

Moments later, some light crept through the blinds, and she's never forgotten that sliver of sun since. Opening her eyes to see light making itself known in a sunless room and warming her cheek, this felt like hope. Where she was from, she never had to hunt for the sun. Sure it would rain and get dreary here and there, but the sun now appeared so distant, like it never wanted to come out. It hid behind buildings and tiptoed around clouds. She wondered if it was her own dreariness taking over. The truth was that this was the first time in months she had noticed a burst of light. It made her wonder. It couldn't have been more than a little after six, and the clouds usually didn't care to part until seven, so the sun making itself known had to be a sign. She had been taught to decipher these sorts of things. Maybe it was her mother, from wherever she was, giving her the nudge she needed to get up. It could have been the other major player in her life, that gangly woman placing her hands on top of hers to knead the dirt like it was dough. As flickers of light sparkled on her hand, she became alert, feeling her body warm; her hair, her face, her sheets, thank God. In that bed, she was sure she had been found. She watched the end of the sun's ray halt at the base of the opposite wall, ready to begin the day.

She parted her hair down the middle, forming each section into two braids. Wore a pair of earrings and large costume jewelry pearls bought at a gas station. The earrings were heavy, and she worried that someone might notice her lobes were drooping. Better for them to focus on her fake pearls than her protruding belly. She still wore her ring and his last name, but if any questions came her way asking for specifics she'd be safer buried under the covers. These were the things that preoccupied her lately, whether someone would unveil her discomfort. The plaited hair, drooping pearls, and the hidden belly were what she took with her to the interview for a job as an assistant in an office.

It would be this day she'd remember from the haze of how rapidly life was shifting. Moments that would have been commemorative to anyone else were becoming a list of events scribbled into a ring-bound turquoise planner. The day she vomited the porridge into the toilet. September 4, 1976. The departure of Usen-the-so-called-Samuel. October 17, 1976. Her Advanced Chemistry II exam. November 10, 1976. The flimsy planner was proof that she was moving forward.

She'd flip through the lined pages to admire her notations. If the only leverage she had over her situation was momentum, then she'd let that mighty force propel her deeper into the void that was closing in. Maybe she'd even find joy there.

But what she recalled the most was her encounter with the perfumed lady who smelled like she had walked through a carwash raining down cinnamon. Mrs. Hall.

The woman, wearing an otherwise agreeable scent now turned noxious fume, sat behind the desk scanning her pointer finger across Uduak's resume. A late-sixty-something-year-old who had been the HR manager for ten years and insisted that a jar of peanut M&M's remain in the corner of the front desk for those wanting to crunch on something nutty. She had fired the previous assistant for putting out a bowl of regular M&M's for those allergic to peanuts. Her greatest ally, Mr. Hall, the now deceased high school biology teacher and beloved football coach, would have understood why she nixed the previous assistant. He'd also get why she could never hire the candidate in front of her. He had always lauded her straitlaced attitude and traditional mores as a virtue in need of restoration. One night he griped about how the changes of the last decade were bulldozing the past without any regard for those who needed an adjustment window before they could ride the wave. He said, "If this is what it means to live in 1976 then take me out of it." The next day a stroke took him. His wife, ever faithful to her nature, placed a blue urn with an inscription of his name in silver by her bedside and a week later marched into her office ready to hire a worthy assistant. A Hall would never stay brooding over what God saw fit to take away, and so she sat dutifully at her post, surveying the paper in front of her attempting to pronounce, "You-dak?"

"Uduak, Ma'am."

"Beg your pardon?"

"Uduak."

"Any other names we can call you?"

"No, Ma'am."

"Where you coming from?"

"Westbury, Ma'am."

"Originally?"

"Nigeria, Ma'am."

"Nigeria?"

"Yes, Ma'am."

"Okie doke."

Mrs. Hall prided herself on always being the smartest person in the room, even when sitting beside the hoity-toity science men she worked under. Those men were nothing but numbers, equations, and hot air. Much younger than her too. One prick to their puffed-up egos and they shrank into boys who couldn't work the coffee machine or decide what to eat for lunch. Thirty seconds was all she needed to find out what was brewing inside anybody who came into her view, but when facing this candidate, she couldn't make her out.

What she didn't know was that the young woman was one step ahead, as she had been taught to hear the thing that cannot be heard and see the thing that cannot be seen. Every gesture from Mrs. Hall was a clue. The way the prim and proper lady's eyes skipped about, using her mouth to say a bunch of low mhmms, and high okie dokes! with lags between phrases that seemed to skirt around an unspeakable something-she-wouldn't-dare-say-but-in-fact-should-say-because-her-not-saying-it-was-causing-them-both-distress. And back to those eyes, how they kept shifting about with her blunders when trying to say "You-duck??" But it didn't matter how Mrs. Hall tried to hide. Uduak could hear what she was really thinking.

What would he think about this?

The paper came down a tad, enough for their eyes to meet, and Uduak tried to make her case.

"Ma'am, I'm a hard worker."

"Thank you for coming in. You'll hear from me in a week." Mrs. Hall said this quickly, eager to end her guilt.

Uduak would never forget this woman's real name, a name for what those fast eyes and slow mouth gave away. *Mbu buk*. And it was then that she knew she'd have a baby girl. A decision made out of spite. Perhaps this was the only time she had overrode the will of some higher fate, but giving birth to a better version of herself would show them all. If her child turned out the way she intended, this child would get even with all the people who had doubted her. And this is what they had done, all of them, in one way or another. They may have argued that they hadn't considered how bad the situation could get. They may have tried to save face somehow, saying, "Now see, you would have come to us about this before things escalated . . . ," a rubbish excuse like that. This daughter would be prettier, quicker, stronger, and lovelier, this is what she'd be. This is what she had to be. Otherwise, they were finished.

Her lot was unfortunate, and soon she'd have to accept that her sojourn had become a calamity. She had come up short, which made her desire for another part of herself all the more clear. It would be a slice of herself that could show a better portrayal of her efforts, which in that moment felt deeply insignificant, because who would want to sing the praises of an educated woman begging for a scrap from someone refusing to hold a gaze with her? No one would want to hear this type of wretched account back home. The glory doesn't belong to the woman haplessly toiling in obscurity waiting for something to bloom. Everyone knows that.

God, give me the daughter I need, and I will love her. This was her silent prayer in the office where she tried not to exhale for fear of inhaling the death smell the lady in front of her had worn. A smell that made it impossible for her to hold her composure. The vision of a better child consoled her as she said, "Thank you for your time," and then realized she had breathed too much of the woman's stench in.

This daughter of hers would be her firstborn, and as the firstborn, she'd even know how to sneeze better than her. One might think this a strange thought for a soon-to-be-Mum-of-a-better-daughter, but it was the most appropriate thought she could muster as she covered her hands over her nose, sneezing snot and rage into her palms.

The first thing everyone saw was a cotton-like texture inching out of her down-there parts. She wondered if she was witnessing the handiwork of a disgruntled ancestor putting a hex on her for doing everything she had been taught not to do since she had left home. She couldn't let herself believe that it was God (the One who brought the world Christ, of course) who would hurt her in this way. Surely, He heard her prayers when she put her trust in the sacred tenet, ask and ye shall receive. It gave her pause that a possible divination had occurred to frustrate her efforts. She winced at such a dark thought but also accepted she had left a country filled to the brim with a people's frustration. It could have been the handiwork of a family member consulting with a spiritual advisor and then that spiritual advisor doing a ritual to invoke the spirits from the other side to chase her for not keeping a leaving husband, wanting a diploma more than a family, and returning to her father's compound with a jutting belly. Some people had been fooled into believing there needed to be at least three people to start a family, but she was certain that it could start with two. And it didn't have to be a man and woman arm in arm helming the catastrophe. And that's what her situation was—a catastrophe.

She examined the fluffiness and hoped any ancestor with a gripe didn't wield too much power. It wasn't all the ancestors you had to agree with or even like, anyway. Her grandma was someone she listened to when required, but now that the old woman had gone, she found comfort in admitting that her experiences with her were mostly insufferable. But too bad she died before the matter of her broken marriage could be resolved. Grandma had put the onus on her daughter and son-in-law to free Uduak from the clutch of propriety for all their sakes. They had shoved her granddaughter into the union, and they should have been the ones to pull her out. These were her last wishes uttered to everyone who came into view, but everyone in her view was quietly wishing for the frail woman to die because her yammering revealed their culpability, bringing to light that they didn't want to step in. They, the brothers, sisters, father, mother, uncles, aunts, distant relatives, and spiritual advisors all wanted the marriage to stay intact. And they didn't want to feel bad about it.

They knew the overarching details, sympathized even, but they wanted the young wife to forgive and let it go. Seventy times seventy-seven times if she had to. In that hospital bed, without someone to hold her hand, the new mother hoped that she wasn't giving birth to a devil child.

She began to pray when a nurse asked, "Are you alright?"

Another nurse asked, "What language is she speaking?"

"Wouldn't know. Shift's almost over, anyway. Where's Elaine?"

It was then that Uduak realized she was praying in her language and that it was night outside. She had hoped for a day baby, but who can really time these things?

A choir of hmms, oohs, and huhs sang in the hospital room, making a melodic assertion that none of this seemed possible. The doctor put everyone at ease when he confirmed what the stuff coming out her canal was. "Hair," he said.

The more pressing thing that didn't seem possible was that the actual pushing out of the baby didn't hurt. The cushion of hair made it feel like pushing out a pillow with legs. She wondered if everything she had heard about childbirth was true, but then considered that the whole event might be a hallucination.

A cooing girl with a smooth face and a full head of hair was in her arms. And with eyes stretching so wide they left little space for a nose and mouth. The other pressing thing was the girl was quiet. No scream marked the occasion of a baby. No cry of indignation at being thrust from the warm cave that held her for nine months. Not even a whimper.

Uduak parted the baby's coils and pressed the softness beneath her palm. The baby yawned and rested herself against her breast and all seemed well as she rubbed her tiny fingers. She kissed her forehead and uttered the word that spoke most succinctly to the moment, "Welcome." The mother's eyelids closed as she lulled herself to sleep with her thoughts. *Ekpewan.* But then she thought of the child's hair, the first idea she got was to cut it.

The child looked at the mother in what appeared to be dismay. Her cheeks cooled and the baby arched its head back as it let out a sob.

The Outing

The United States, 2012. Arit.

The dream goes something like this. I'm seated at a majestic banquet table, gasping for air but doing my best to hide my asphyxiation. The corset I'm wearing is squeezing the dignity out of me, but since I look good, I bear it.

I see French macarons, broccoli slathered in Velveeta cheese, fruit punch, hamburger pizza, a pot of white sugar, garlic fries, biscuits, chocolate-covered donuts, evaporated milk, chin-chin, orange soda, petit fours, Lipton tea, red wine, Philly cheesesteaks, and a vat of sour cream on the dining table. These are the foods of my childhood and early twenties. I indulged in these foods for comfort. If I couldn't fix a problem, at least I could eat my way through it. I still get cravings from time to time. Whenever I bite into sautéed kale with garlic, I find myself chanting, *this is a buttered biscuit, this is a buttered biscuit, this is a buttered biscuit.* No surprise that I'm seeing a bounty of biscuits in this dream.

My family and our guests sit at the table. The women wear dresses with muted colors that are quite drab. The men banter back and forth, duking it out for the title of Most Clever. Their collars are tight around their necks, and I fear they're choking but don't know it. Servants walk briskly about the dining hall to bring us food and drink. They look like blurs really, but I know they are there. My father sits at the head of the table, Mom's seated beside him, and there are random people I've never met, which makes me wonder if I should know them.

My father clinks his glass to propose a toast. He's donned a super-sized Afro that distracts me from his speech. In a crowd full of Victorian wigs, how's this Afro going to pan out? He looks more suited to attend the Soul Train Awards or bite his thumb at the monarchy, but who am I to judge? I stuff my face hoping to disappear.

Eating beats talking. I wouldn't even know what to say, or how to say it anyway. A voice is a powerful impression and I'm at a loss for which to use. Should I use the British English my parents speak in polite company or the pidgin they speak in exasperation? Should I use my standard American voice, fit with a slight Bostonian mumble, or use the voice needed when I'd like to mollywop somebody's ass? Maybe I should speak the language my parents spoke back home, though I don't know it; everyone assumes English isn't my first language anyway. Maybe then

I should use the voice I use with myself. Jittery and hard to pin down.

"Lady Arit has a message to report tonight. I've heard that it's a salacious secret, and though I detest scandal, I think it is best her ladyship reveal what's at hand here." Everyone looks at me as if I'll soon be served for the main course.

"Yes, Arit," Mom says, taking a drink of wine. "We are most eager to hear this secret of yours. But before you divulge, allow me to say that nothing hides in the company of a prayer warrior." The guests break into laughter.

"Don't fret over Lady Arit's peculiar disposition. She's taking precautions to ensure she'll relay the message wisely."

My father clears his throat.

"Hurry now before our good meal goes cold," he barks.

I look at my reflection in the spoon and see it's an image of another woman. I refuse to name her, but she shakes her head and laughs through the brass. *Better say the truth.* The audience leans in. I knock a pitcher of wine to the ground. The wine coats the floor until it becomes a pool of red. I scoop the wine and realize it's much thicker than expected and the smell is metallic. Blood?

I quickly remember who I am in my waking life, but this thought doesn't soothe, because even if the wigs and accents were gone, I'm not sure there'd be much of a difference.

I began having this dream after Mom's phone call. When she confronted me she asked, "Are you engaging in woman-to-woman practices?"

The best I could answer was, "Never ruled it out."

She was relieved that the possibility of my dating the opposite sex wasn't ruled out, but this relief perturbed me.

"Please don't say I'm completely *this* when I'm not sure I'm fully *that*." I was shrill and whiny as I spoke. No bass, all flutter.

"How'd you find out?" I asked.

"You posted a picture. You know I like to investigate. . . were you hiding all this time?"

"I don't think so," I answered. "I didn't think this would be such a crime."

Mom let out a hiss.

"My dear, back where I come from, it is."

She called the next day in a series of threes. Interrupting me during my job hunt. Three times in the morning. Three times in the afternoon. Three times at night. Her fixation with the number started with her love of all things Jesus Christ. Once she read the passage about how Jesus—the Son—belonged to the Father and the Holy Ghost, she believed everything had to belong to something. Three became her obsession. If she bought fruit, she had to buy the navel oranges, the purple grapes, *and* the bananas because they belonged in the polka-dotted fruit bowl. If she was dressing me for church, she made sure I wore the itchy white lace dress, with the black Mary Janes and that hideous striped sweater because according to her, consistency in attire would put me closer to God. I've always feared her relationship with Him; it seemed to override my pleas when trying to get her attention. I would yank her arm, hoping she would look down, but she was always looking up, forever preoccupied with a higher power.

Exactly three days later, she phoned again, letting me know where I stood with her and God. *We didn't raise you this way.* I began ignoring her calls, but then the guilt took hold. I've watched plenty of bizarre movies where mothers put arsenic in your chicken noodle soup to collect insurance, or sleep with your boyfriend, or beat you because they're threatened. This was the woman who worked the graveyard shift to make a down payment on a house in a nicer neighborhood. She once hid from a man pounding the door saying, "Open this now."

"He had a gun," she'd told me. "Thank goodness that door was locked."

She had been pregnant with me.

I took the call.

"Remove that picture dear. I'm begging," she said. "They use social media back home, too. You'll never get to visit in peace if they see this about you."

The following week I skipped her calls though I couldn't stop the voice repeating, *I love her. I love her. I love her.*

She left messages. They were deadly but she probably thought she was doing me a favor. I pronounced the week: The Week of Holy Venom.

Monday

"Isn't it too much of the same thing? The same part bumping against the same part?" she asked, knowing I wasn't there. "You're such a pretty girl. Please, don't let it go to waste."

Tuesday

She read from the Bible. "'Behold, this was the iniquity of thy sister Sodom, pride, fullness of bread, and abundance of idleness was in her and in her daughters, neither did she strengthen the hand of the poor and needy. And they were haughty, and committed abomination before me: therefore I took them away as I saw no good.'"

Wednesday

She sang.

Akwa convention
Odu ke edem eyon
Nyin ikwo iyun idara
Koro Jehovah odong
Nyin esit

Loose translation: You're going to hell.

Thursday

"I've been thinking deeply about your cousin Minnie. I'm sure you've seen on Facebook that she likes to practice this woman-to-woman thing . . ."

I took a sip of tea with a shot of whiskey and wondered, where is this going?

"Arit, you don't have to copy what Minnie is doing. Okay?"

I haven't spoken to Minnie in five years.

Friday

She breathed into the receiver before saying anything.

I waited.

"Is it because you lost your job? You've been sounding different. Come home. Please."

Saturday

"Should I tell your father?" she asked, though her question didn't feel like an ask. "I don't like keeping secrets."

I closed my mouth and screamed.

Sunday

"I love you."

"It's pure theater!" Nkechi eagerly listened to Mom's messages while scarfing down a bean burrito. "She's an artist, but then again, what Nigerian mother isn't?"

After nights of swimming in blood and drowning, I told her everything.

"What picture did she see, anyway?" Nkechi asked.

"That one where I was wearing the rainbow skirt with the reindeer antlers."

"Got it." She nodded. "No one should call you out for wearing a rainbow. How sacrilegious."

"I don't know what to do."

"Do *you*, boo." She sat back and swallowed her last bite. "They don't pay for your flights to visit, and they don't buy your hair."

"I'll keep eating carbs until I feel better."

"Don't become a sadomasochist, girl. Eating that way makes you sick. Just tell the truth."

"I'm not sure what truth to tell."

She flashed me a glance and took a sip of Coke. "You do."

Nkechi. She had a Grace Jones haircut and wore those three-dollar biker shorts bought at our favorite thrift store the day I wore the rainbow. She threw glitter at random folks for a good hour, cackling while she did it, flinging the stuff like there was something to prove. I wondered why she had to do extra when we were already in a parade with music blasting and people yelling into bullhorns. I wanted to wear my skirt and rest in the cacophony, but here she was, wanting to orchestrate it. I was perturbed with her a little, but then someone came and wrapped me in a feather boa and I left her to herself.

She's disruptive in her family too. Once, she barged in on her family during a prayer (her family prays like they're in the last days too) and said, "Look, don't expect any children 'cause nothing is coming out this cooch and don't expect a husband 'cause marriage is for fools." She then said, "And don't try talking me out of it. We're in America, and I'm gonna suck all the power I can from this country before I twirl back to Naija."

After much silence, her Mom—Mrs. Duruji— said, "Your choice of dress shows that you are of a flamboyant variety. I only pray that life isn't too hard for you. It's hard enough."

I wouldn't have believed this story, that her parents were this accepting, but she still lives at home, parties late into the night, changes her hair every two weeks, and smokes weed in the house (but only in her room with the window open).

I never understood why everyone expected Nigerians to be so dramatic until I met this family and thought I had entered a Nollywood movie.

Mrs. Duruji wears a mid-length blonde wig that she combs every forty-five minutes to ensure her hair doesn't tangle. She has a heap of wigs to "elevate" herself, Shirley Temple curls, Cher tresses, and the Tina Turner shag. Nkechi has one, an Angela Davis fro. Her Mom says it's unbecoming, especially if working an office job. Says it's not lady-like. Nkechi pays her no mind, says, "You know I'm no lady and when you were my age neither were you."

She knows at least three good secrets about her Mom. Can you believe that?

"I wish your life would rub off on mine," I told her.

"What does that mean?" she asked.

"You know who you are. I worry so much that I don't know if I'm anything other than the worry."

"That's you getting laid off talking. Once you start making money again, you'll be alright."

"It's been rough. For a while."

"Why you think that is?"

"Someone must be pissed at me."

"Someone's pissed at you?" She laughed, in disbelief.

"Can you quiet down?" I said, noticing some people sitting nearby staring.

"Oh I forgot it." Nkechi rolled her eyes, getting louder. "Laughing's beneath you."

"It's not funny."

"It is funny. You're like my Mom. Always griping about someone trying to cast a spell on her because they're angry. You both need to stop. Things ain't working here? Go where it will."

"Where's that?"

"Home. That's what I did when I couldn't make rent. Went home and my parents were too glad to have me."

"I'd have to go somewhere else."

"If you won't go home then at least stay here," she said. "Maybe it's better to stay close to the devil you know."

"I'm not like you at all."

Nkechi flashed me another look, a bit softer. "I'll probably be that weird aunt everyone loves but secretly thinks, wow, her life is ruined. That's the role they've cast me in. I could never do what you've done. Leave my family? Leave my mother? No," she said. "You're brave."

I laughed in utter disbelief. "Brave?" I almost shrieked.

"All I feel is grief."

Where I come from, fervent prayer is the cure for all human folly. When Aunty Nancy heard about Uncle Emem's porn addiction, she sent him away to a motel, packed up her rambunctious children, and drove from Hartford, Connecticut, to my Mom's prayer circle. It was held once a month for women wanting to link arms in prayer. They were women I remember meeting at a banquet hall for people like us, people who were coming from the same state my parents grew up in. They needed a respite from sticking out like sore thumbs and got dressed to gather somewhere they could feel normal. They were heavily perfumed in gardenia or musk dabbed on the nape of their necks, in the crevice of their elbows and on their inner thighs. They painted their lips hot pink or blood red with jewelry draping from their ears and wrists. Mom rubbed me down with Vaseline that day. Took rollers out of my hair till it sat in a James Brown coiffure and had me wear those wretched itchy white tights. These were the same women who came to the prayer circle. They prayed morning, noon, and night. I barely knew the home language—the language they prayed in—but was frightened by this mysterious power of invocation they harnessed.

When my aunt visited, I relished the way us children were allowed to play freely. We'd tiptoe through the parlor where our mothers linked arms and bowed their heads, rustle for food in the kitchen, and then dash for the yard with a handful of chin-chin, howling into the forest. Our voices echoed through the tall oak trees as we impersonated superheroes. If my father had seen me, I would have been spanked for not being a good girl, which to him meant remaining quiet and watchful. To have a daughter yelling in a neighborhood where people walked their dogs, rode their bikes, and took note of everything was an embarrassment.

Thankfully, the women praying somehow managed to keep his temper at bay. He'd simply grunt, "Call me when the room is cleared," and retreat to his room.

Uncle Emem returned a few weeks later, promising he'd give up his habit and rededicate his life to Christ. Mom was convinced their prayers had made the difference, but I think it was the fact that Aunty Nancy kicked him out, cut him off from his children, and was the breadwinner of the family. When Mom's father was diagnosed with brain cancer, she flew to Nigeria to pray for him. Her family prayed every day at 9 a.m., noon, and 3 p.m. for two weeks straight.

Grandpa died a month later, and for some reason Mom still prays for his recovery. She believes everyone needs a good word, whether they're dead or living.

Mom prayed for my human folly too. When I was in high school, I took to wearing halter tops. After she caught me I had to wear long-sleeved shirts in ninety-degree weather.

That night I was headed upstairs when I heard her praying in her room. Between words from the home language and bits of English she said, "Arit—make her good, Father. Make her good . . ."

A terrible feeling took over, a feeling that someone had cast a spell behind my back. She gave God a message about who I was without any chance of me stating my piece. I realized that she had something over me, something that could very well kill me if I wasn't careful—conviction. She would most likely pray about my heathen tendencies before jumping in to stop a hand from slapping my face.

If I had my own direct line to Him I'd say, "This woman keeps interfering with my nature, and I don't know what to do."

I eat an enormous number of macarons with no taste. I can't describe what nothing tastes like. It's more of a feeling. I devour more cookies, eat through the blandness, grab the fuschia macaron, then a green, a tangerine, a blue. I devour until I hear her.

"How dare you blacken our good name with such scandal," Mom says this, taking a bite of Charlotte Russe.

I look down at my place setting. A pile of cookies sitting on a plate. A soup spoon is there, and a woman smiles at me through it. I'm alarmed because she's trapped inside but doesn't seem to know it. She reaches her hand through the spoon. "Hand me a macaron, girl. This gonna be a long night." I give her the yellow, I can't taste it but I enjoy it the least.

"Well," Mom says. "What do you have to say for yourself?"

I look down at the woman in the spoon chomping away. "Just tell them," she says. "Tell them." She finishes the cookie. "Doesn't it taste good?" she asks, delighted. I nod my head in agreement, not knowing why. I then get some taste from the bits of cookie in my mouth. Dirt. It tastes like dirt.

Here are three things I don't like about Nkechi. One. She's stupid. Or maybe she's psycho, but whatever she is, I find myself looking at her and thinking she's a disaster. She can never walk herself back to sanity after crossing the line. I'll never forget that time she walked the streets with lime green spandex, a crop top, and four-inch heels. She walked like this through the Tenderloin, the Haight, the Financial District, and the Castro. Past whistling men, past haughty women, past children, past police officers, past the wind, past the rain, past the sun, and past all reason. I offered her a sweater but she refused.

"Stop worrying all the time," she said. "You got to rise above the foolery, girl. Whether you live or die."

Two. She's a shit starter. Last week we were waiting at the BART and a shifty-looking man bumped into her. She snapped. "I'm standing here, idiot." It was eleven at night, we had just passed a man shooting up into his leg as we walked down the steps, and I had no interest in losing my life inside a train station. She knew this, but she didn't care. This man didn't scare me one bit. He wouldn't be the first shifty man I survived. But she—Nkechi—frightened me that day.

He was foul, the man, and he started talking. *Fuck you, you bitch this, you Black this, you c*!% this, you roach this . . .*

I motioned for her to cool it.

"You don't want none of dis at this unholy hour. Dude, I will cut you," she said.

He got closer.

"If he touches you, I'll hurt him!" I said. "Walk away."

His attention turned towards me. *Fuck you, you bitch this, you Black this, you c*!% this, you roach this.*

She heckled in his direction. "I will fling you across this platform. No joke."

He spat. Threw his entire head back to do it and the blob landed on her arm.

She looked hurt, like she could whimper. I stepped in. Slapped him. Twice. He held his cheek and went somewhere.

"All the things we got to live with in this country," she said, rustling for a napkin in her backpack. "I should have kicked him in the balls. He lucky I'm not that fucked up on Jack."

I handed her a napkin from my purse.

"You were livid," she said, wiping her arm. "He's a loser but don't you think you were too hard on him?"

I was certain I hated her then.

Three. She knows I don't like her. I can love a thing, but not really like that same thing. I love her because she reminds me of home and she knows me from the inside out. She's gotten the closest, out of all of them, even more than any lover I've had.

Up until three days ago, I was with someone named Jamal. A brother who always wears a five o'clock shadow. I considered sending a picture of us to Mom, hoping she'd accept this part of me. But then Jamal decided to pop up at my apartment with a hamburger pizza. He was proud of his attempt at surprise but all I could ask myself was, who raised him?

"We're getting older, you're gonna need memories that involve you actually staying the course." Nkechi said.

Then she mentioned the girl I dated a few months back, Sarah Jane. A high-brow type from Napa Valley. She defied her father's expectations by working at a shelter. Nkechi hated how vanilla she was, but since it got me out on Friday nights, she soon approved. We had met at some professional event. She kept calling, I finally gave in, we began dating. Two months later she wanted to take me for lunch with her best friend, Martha. I ended it a day later. Nkechi asked why, and I said, "Her name doesn't fit."

To love a thing but not like a thing is perfectly sane in this kinda world. A world where people love but don't like, or like but don't love, or simply hate. I was a quiet girl. A shy girl. Meek. That was me. I didn't want to hurt nobody. I just wanted to be who I was, whatever *that* was, but in this trip of a world. I'm lucky. Lucky I'm anything at all. It started with the day someone looked my way and said, *you're pretty*. It was a curse. Don't care what nobody says about the beautiful finishing first. It was. After that, the voices never stopped.

You pretty. Listen well. Pretty girls kiss men. Strong men. Big men. Like that one there. Wait. Not him. He White. He White? We don't want no wahala now. Too much to explain. Find a Black. African-born Black. They'll understand you. Don't make him angry. Remember. Divorce is a sin. And you pretty. So pretty. Wait. You not pretty. Blacky. Lips too big. Hair too coiled. Ass too small. And you frown. Why frown? You pretty. So pretty. Wait. Why wear that? Show your legs. They nice. Wait. Why show your body? You a whore? Whore. Wait. You pretty. So pretty. Why wear baggy clothes? Wear a dress. Why you crying? Don't cry. You sensitive. Stop. Wait. I love you. Why you silent? Speak. But speak smart. Wait. Shut up. What you say? You too loud. No one will listen now. You fucked up. Wait. I adore you. Where's my credit? For loving you?

"Well?" Mom says. "What do you have to say for yourself?" I look from her to the woman in the spoon watching me intently. "I'm not sure I love any of you."

The woman inside the spoon vanishes.

Part 2

Clothed in my dignity,
the only worthy garment,
I go my way

—Mariam Ba

Aggie

Kenya, 2018. Arit.

Haven't you met those women who smile, flashing a rack of teeth, but you get an inkling that what they're really flashing are their fangs? I liken it to those 1950s housewives who smiled over a knife slicing meatloaf and decades later what do we have? We have numerous books and movies about how these women were cutting their wrists, plotting their escapes, writing their manifestos, and scheming to put a knife in someone's back. Usually, it's the back of the person they kept smiling at until they could smile no more. I don't know how to Africanize the aforementioned example here, but some looks are truly universal, and it's this smiling-while-wielding-a-deadly-weapon face that Aggie wore. She was a woman who messed with my rhythm, jumbled the delicate pacing of my life, taking my stability.

I'd warn anyone against striking a friendship while the other party is half asleep. So when she opened the sliding door at 3 a.m. and said, "There's my friend," I gave her a strike for assuming such un-earned familiarity. I was clear on who I was that night: A hypervigilant woman who had skipped her ticket back to the US to travel until her visa ran out. My standoffishness was to ward off the wrong per-son: a date rapist, an axe murderer, a kidnapper, a human trafficker, those beach boys who become like Velcro when they realize you're alone, or a random man twice your age believing that a single woman dining alone in Mombasa is hungry for a sugar daddy.

As of late, my biggest fear was meeting sloppy drunks binging on two-for-one Mojito deals at the happy hour. Liquor and a broken heart are a terrible mix, and the people who frequented the hostel bar would get enough sauce in them to groan about the one who left and the misery that followed.

My goal was to sit by the beach in a nearby hotel and wait for a message because I had believed the water could talk. So let me assuage any doubts about my reliability and say yes, I possibly have lost my mind. I've taken my pills—Seroquel, Xanax, Zoloft—to keep tethered to this plane, to ignore that voice that once said, *I could have been you.* If it takes admitting that I possibly heard someone at some time speak to me, and that now, I wait to hear from her, then fine.

It was in front of the Indian Ocean, that I heard a voice erupt in a wave saying, "When are you gonna say what happened?" It was the only message I had received in years and this propelled me to go and wait for another message to roll in. That was a Saturday, and since I can no longer tell Monday from Thursday and Friday from Sunday, the reason I know the voice came in on this day was due to the hotel's bulletin board that read "Saturday Reggae Night for the New Year." A martini glass was drawn in chalk, with three olives on a toothpick and a man holding the glass, smiling brightly with a talking bubble at the corner of his mouth reading, *yum*, and I thought, whoever drew this had too much time to blow through and was attempting to fill each moment before all was lost. Christmas was one big party that leaked into the next day and the next. In a place where people come and go, bulletin boards are often erased as new announcements are made, and the constant rotation of new faces makes life fleeting. And yet, that message on the board anchored me somehow, a woman on the coast traveling alone who would likely never attend a Saturday reggae night.

I returned to the dorm with sand funk on my heels and red eyes only to wrestle with the water the following day. I wasn't too vexed in my soul to be in hell, but I was disturbed enough about the state of my affairs to consider the day-in and day-out of sand, leery drunkards, and the silence from the water to be a kind of purgatory. And I met Aggie this way, waiting for a message.

She wore a dress with a hat that reminded me of church ladies, judgment, and the tide coming in. A patch of violet flowers against navy blue fabric showed on her dress as the tiki torch light rested on her hem. The navy blue was the color of a mailbox, jogging a memory of dropping a letter in a box that read, *outgoing*. If she had worn a hat and placed three white feathers at the side, it would have been Sunday morning. I was not impressed.

I was shocked that Marura, the stalwart front-desk manager with the wide forehead, hadn't given me a heads up. Her ability to monitor the comings and goings of everything concerning the Sunshine Breeze Hostel while swiftly enforcing the "no walk-ins from 1 a.m. to 7 a.m." rule had secured her the coveted status of star staff. She was so revered that it was like her feet never touched the ground. A German man who rented a single with his Kenyan lover called her God, laughing that God was a Kenyan woman by the water shepherding a crew of degenerates and lost souls in need. The patrons tipped her well, saying she should be running the place. Two hoteliers tried poaching her, enticing her with an upper management position, an office with an A/C, and access to whatever she wanted on the regular menu instead of the staff food. Far as I know, the red carpet was rolled out for her more than for any local I've known. She had flexible work hours and a son who often used the pool at the hostel, so she declined all offers. Politely though. That was Marura, riding the edge of a sergeant's formality with a tinge of sweetness. This woman clocked almost everything, from one minute to the next, she was good.

I prided myself on being more together than the patrons who lost themselves at the front desk, revealing the most despicable details of their lives to a stranger. The gossip about Stan the swinger who treated his flings to the pancake breakfast at the hostel restaurant, Marura knew. The housekeeper who picked the pockets of the patrons taking the single room, she knew. The waitresses who got fired for partying with the guests, she knew. Without her, the Sunshine Breeze Hostel would have been exposed for the candy cane operation it was. How'd she miss this? How'd she miss Aggie? My anger at Aggie's entrance was propelled by my bewilderment with the manager's oversight.

In fact, my anger with this entire situation may truly reside with Marura, but she is entirely untouchable. Everyone has dragged themselves to the front desk at one point or another, divorcées, sex addicts, widowers, potheads, travelers on mission trips burdened with saving the planet, and your functional depressives. She'd offer limited advice that was in line with the happy-go-lucky airs the hostel displayed for everyone. She'd review her manicured nails (I say review because it seemed like she was always searching for perfection in her fingers) that were usually painted black and then look at the customer, read them the company policy, and say, "It'll all be sawa*, tomorrow." I hadn't heard her say more than this, unless she was giving information or speaking on the phone with her son. The esteem I held her in embarrassed me, it was inappropriate to

*A popular Swahili word that means okay

127

treat her as if she was made of pixie dust. I'd have denounced this in most circumstances, asserting her right to be ordinary flesh and blood, but I needed her to tell me who was entering my space—and she should have known because she always knew.

Aggie didn't look like a traveler who had taken two matatus to rent an $11-a-night bed. Most folks lug oversized backpacks and wear sturdy sandals that wrap around the ankle for extra support. Their feet are covered in dust and they have rings of dirt under their nails. After twenty-four hours of transiting, eating street food, and taking pictures, whether or not they're coming from Ecuador, South Africa, Denmark, Spain, or Japan, they smell like a ripe armpit. And they flaunt their odor shamelessly, because after all they're roughing it in Africa. They'll inhale a quick bite, go to a party, get wasted, and have sex without concern for the stench wreaking from their privates. Her perfume filled the room with a fruity scent, though I couldn't place the fruit. Clearly, she wasn't one of them.

"I'm Aggie," she said. "Can I turn on the light? I won't be long."

The tiki lights shone through the glass. The soundtrack always playing at the bar flooded the dorm with percussive bass lines and a mellow tempo for travelers and locals to meet over a shot of Jack Daniels, grilled meat, cigarettes, and a late-night swim. Something about her appeared filled to the brim and in need of air, like tightly packed flour. It wasn't her size, it was the way she carried it, with

128

her dress waving from side to side. A twinge of jealousy shot through me, as I had no girth to switch across a room and had always wished I had something visible to wield when I walked through the door.

I responded evenly, "Okay."

I turned my back to her and faced the wall.

In the daylight Aggie looked familiar. She had the toothy smile of my sister, the chipmunk cheeks of that cousin who used to hide my shoes, and the plum skin of my brother. I had finished eating breakfast (two sausages, toast, a fried egg, and mixed tea) for 500 bob and then went to my room to sit under the air conditioner. At 9 a.m. the heat was unbearable. I had sat on the couch for ten minutes until I heard a shuffle in the corner. There she was sprawled across the bed in white shorts and a peplum top writing in a pocket-sized spiral notebook, which I guessed must have been her diary as I had a tattered leather journal in a shoebox that I put under my bunk bed and I had been writing in it for three years. She held it in a way that let me know the tiny book was precious to her somehow, important. There was a woman scribbling away, unaware of another presence in the room, and I warmed up to her then, remembering that those of us who don't say much have much to say.

"Where are you coming from?" I asked.

"Nairobi."

"So you're on vacation?"

She leaned back a touch. "Yeah. And you?"

"On holiday, I guess. A long one."

"From where?"

"America."

"Oh. When did you move there?"

"I was born and raised there."

"You?"

"Yes."

"Oh . . . so you're an African born in America and now you're visiting here which makes you a Black American. Makes sense."

"Yeah."

"But you are African, right? You're not like one of those who forget . . ."

"Don't think so."

"You're Nigerian, right?"

"Yes."

"You look like it."

"Okay."

"What? You don't like that you look the way your people look?"

"Oh no. I like that."

"Good. That's good. Because then how else can you know who you are if you don't want to look like your people? Right?"

I didn't answer.

She sat up to get a better look. "Well, you aren't loud like your people. Nigerians always have to have their way—so aggressive—but you all have the best music by far. You have got us beat there. But with the way you carry yourself, you could pass for one of us. Since when have you been here?"

"Three weeks," I answered.

"You're traveling alone?"

"Sure," I said.

"And you're not lonely?"

I shook my head no.

"I didn't catch your name?"

"Arit."

"And your native name?"

"Arit. Yours?"

"Wangechi."

A tiny scratch rested between her nose and mouth. I doubt anyone would have caught that. Who knows what she noticed on me.

"And your family?" she asked.

"In the States. Yours?"

"Dead."

"Dead?"

"My parents. I'm an only child. So when will you go back?"

"Back where?"

"To America."

"I'm not sure when I'll go back home."

"Home? But isn't America so stressful? That country likes killing Black people too much! You really think that's your home?"

"Yes."

"Will you visit Nigeria?"

"No."

"Why not?"

"I couldn't see myself there."

"But yet you can see yourself in America, where they like killing Black people? That place is definitely not on the list of places I want to go."

"Alright then . . ." I looked at my skirt and saw a ketchup stain dried at the hem in a perfect circle. Had she seen that?

"Come now, it's too much secret-this, secret-that in this room," she said. "This is Mombasa. Time to drink. With the state of your country, Africa must be the safest place on earth to lose one's manners."

I offered for us to go to the lounge around six, after some hesitation. The bar had shots for 200 bob making it the cheapest place in town.

Aggie frowned at my forest-green cotton dress with the pockets below the waist and handed me a fuchsia dress with a plunging neckline that stopped above the knees. I suppose the frock was more suitable for an evening at the bar. The glitter circling the plunging neckline reminded me of a disco. "It'll be smart," she said.

I anticipated the mosquitoes ready to suck the blood from my exposed flesh. I'd have to scratch the bites due to my utter lack of self-control and then pick at myself until the bites turned to scabs. I would have explained this, but it dawned on me that she would see the blood-sucking mosquitoes as the price you pay for beauty.

"This isn't Old Town where women dress more covered," she said. "You can show yourself off without too much trouble. You're not so big like me."

Her eyes scanned my body and I tugged at the bottom of my dress hoping to cover more thigh.

"Let me see you." She straightened my shoulders in the way she might have straightened hers.

"Clothes help with this sort of thing," she said, after close observation.

"What do you mean?" I asked.

"Who doesn't drink and dress to forget?"

"Mmm."

"Guy! Come on. You aren't an angel and neither am I, so what's the deal? You'd feel better if you told me what's with you. It's what friends do. We're friends, right?"

"Nothing's going on. Honestly." I said this to placate her, but she was determined.

"I don't believe you for shit," she said. "That diary you have. What's in it?"

I couldn't pin down when she would have seen my journal. I usually wrote as the sun was coming up, when I could catch memories that felt like they could have happened. By 7 a.m., these memories would fade and I'd grow certain that everything in my notebook was a lie. I didn't realize she had seen that.

"What's in it?" she prodded. "It looked like you were torturing yourself with the way you were writing. Why do that to yourself?"

"Do what? Write?" I asked.

"Write about things that hurt you," she said. "Do you want to know what I write about?"

"No."

"I write about all the places I'll visit. Places I've never been to in Africa, Asia, parts of Europe, stuff like that."

I said the only word that could sum up the moment. "Okay."

"I have a husband," she said. "You know that?"

Aggie possessed a maturity I had grown accustomed to seeing while abroad. Many of the women I had met were often married, rearing their children and managing to make a living, and if you weren't one of those women you were in close proximity to someone who was. I had assumed I was younger than all of them until they told me they were in their mid-twenties, or even younger. They knew at least three languages, could cook three meals a day while working a job, and whether they were vain or modest they seemed like they knew something important about being alive that I didn't.

"I've known him since I left my uncle's house."

"Cool," I said, grateful for a change in conversation. "It's nice when you start out as friends."

"Sometimes a friendship is about what the other person can get away with. What that person knows they can do because they know where you came from. Like him. He beats me. You know that?"

"What?"

"You heard me."

"We're about to go for drinks. Let's keep things light."

"You don't believe me."

"Sure I do."

"Liar."

"You don't seem the type."

"The type that what?"

"The type that gets hit."

"Hit? My friend, I said this man *beats*. I get beatings, okay?"

"Show me then."

She giggled until our eyes locked. She pulled up her dress to reveal an imprint on her thigh. Five tentacle-like fingers etched in her skin, wrapping around like a snake in a coil.

"Why?" I asked.

"Why do you think?" she replied. "The man is considered the king of the castle. You kneel before him while he eats, and you wipe him down when he cums before you wipe yourself. He is God and you are what? And what are you to do if your God kicks and punches because there is no one else to kick and punch but you? And stop staring at me like I'm some wilted flower. I'll kill him one day. You'll see. I'll take him out and go where I wanna go."

How Aggie covered her disfigurement so well bewildered me. I could have taken her to Marura who would have given her a tissue if she cried. She'd listen without doing much. That was Marura, neutral about all matters except that of her son. Earlier that morning I had written in my journal, but I didn't bother to show this to Aggie because it was not fresh and to the point like her bruise. What I wrote read like gibberish:

December ?, 2018

The beige cupboards with the paint peeling off the edges have been replaced with shiny oak wood. The counters rotting from water damage are now marble granite. Marble. How does she afford marble? The recession took your job, remember? Last hired, first fired, remember? They took your work and said it was theirs, remember? Now it's retail and teaching kids who write on your evaluation—she's smart but it's hard to understand her. Her voice is weird. It's well deserved, anyway since you're in pasty-faced New England. God bless every African who's weathered the perils of New England.

She says marble's nice, it's new, it's classy, she deserves it, having sworn her soul to the red, white, and blue flag. Why not marble? she declares. Mom. That's what she says, rattling on. The bathtub upstairs with the big gash in the middle leaks no more. Aloe plants, spider plants, bamboo plants, and cactus plants have taken over the living room. The house is a botanical garden, no longer dusty, the house breathes now. It breathes? Was so stuffy when I lived there. Nine. Nine years it's been since I flew away. She pummels me with her talk of change. This room has turned to this, and this room has turned to that, and this spot has been cleared out, and shouldn't I be happy that life is mov-

ing steadily on foot, trotting towards a horizon that leaves us no choice but to forgive?

But wait, I protest. Don't clean my room. Leave the walls the puke yellow color Ekom and I painted, leave the teddy Okon bought me with his piggy bank money between the pillows on the bed, leave the can of Raid I left in the corner by the dresser to kill those centipedes (when I tired of smashing them), and if you find the twenty I stole during my bad streak inside that wool sock then I'm sorry for taking what was yours, but leave it alone so I don't forget who I became in that house. That room was where I danced and had a buddy—a girl, I'm sure you know her?—the one that visited for a good while. That room was where I learned how to kick Dad.

Mom says, "He's getting better." He had it rough too. I agree. God bless every African who's weathered the perils of New England. Amen.

If she does clean it out, I'll have no one but God to verify what went on in that room. And since God does not sit in the sky but stares at me when I look in the mirror, it'll put me in a hard place. But who can escape mirrors and memories, forever?

Don't clean that room. Repeat. Don't clean that room. I danced there.

Do you know I banished a spirit away, there? Only I could see her, and the person she wanted to talk to the most was you, but you didn't hear or see a thing, so she found me. And we couldn't agree on much, not even what to call you. I said Mom, she said Mum, and the war ensued. I corrected her and then she corrected me because one of us had to be wrong, because how can both of us be right in a place where one feels compelled to have the right answer? Only when we flapped our arms like we had wings, or shook our legs, or turned our hips in circles could we come to a truce. But only for an hour or two. Maybe three.

She lurks now. Showed up with a plate of spaghetti trying to get me to eat in a dream. I threw the plate at her head and screamed I don't crave spaghetti anymore. She says I wanna be your friend, that's all. I love you. I tell her, I don't need no friends, especially the skulking ones who loiter in my dreams. Is this what y'all do? I screamed. Spook humans in your downtime? Don't know what I crave now. But Mom, I do wish to pick up that plate and throw it at your head. I'm sure you'd see it then. Can't deny a piping hot plate of pasta hitting you when half your face is sliding off. I should ask who she is to you. But you'd tell me she's no one.

The last word always belongs to her, though. This is the usual between mothers and daughters as mothers are the quicker ones no doubt. They morph from caretaker to woman with little huff. And you're never prepared for when they drop that hallowed title of being a mother. And when she reminds you that she was once a woman like you, the only thing to do is give her the wide berth she requires to cut you. My dear, she says in mild disgust. Have you ever stayed around for something long enough to see it change? And do you know what it takes to give up your country for a new *one? And now you curse me out because I want some marble and plants in my house? Well . . .*

The average American child may bark back, forgetting herself. But not me, she raised me too well. I wouldn't dare. And it's not like anyone here thinks I'm American.

Yours,

Arit

I had guzzled enough alcohol to do the uncouth thing. Ask for another. Until we floated above the bar and then the bar floated with us, but I can swear we were the first to fly. Marura had made her rounds, crossing to meet us. She must have done this if she got the attention of us in the air.

Two empty seats had been left in the middle of the bar when we first arrived, Karibu, a waitress, said. Janet. I believe that was her name. A slender twenty-something with purple braids. We ordered two doubles, said asante, and watched Janet (or was it Kristine?) turn to get them. These shots were infamous at the bar, named the Tonic by the owner, a Japanese man whose girlfriend concocted it to wide acclaim. The drink tasted unassuming, like an orange jolly rancher. After two of those, the buzz snuck in and you'd fly, or maybe sink, one of the two.

"You'll kill him?" I asked.

"Let's not talk about these heavy-heavy topics," she said. I'm sure she said this. "Drink." And she did say this; she had to say this, because not a minute later we insisted on downing more shots. And I thought I was not the drinking type, but I had spent so much time in search of a message that I had decided the best message may be to simply drink and black out. Our voices slurred and I couldn't make out which was mine and which was hers, but isn't it interesting that when you're drunk and flying (or sinking) you have no concern for how anything sounds?

I have a friend in Uganda. She cooks matoke in banana leaves. Tastes nice. Come with me and I'll have her make it for you. Her voice.

I'll gladly eat matoke, but what will we do over there? And why don't the Ugandans I know like to speak Swahili? My voice.

We'll start over. And not everyone in East Africa likes Swahili. Hers.

I'll deal with my stuff after I leave that place. Mine?

I've rented the room for a few days more. Only a few. Could have been either of us.

I'll tell you everything.

Don't. I have eyes to see. Should I take it off your hands?

What?

Your journal. We can switch.

I'm afraid.

Of what?

Starting over.

We ordered sukuma wiki with rice, a margherita pizza, and complained about there not being dessert on the menu. To make up for this I must have ordered another appetizer because the waitress placed chips masala on the table.

Marura must have swum to make her rounds again because she whispered in my ear to ask if I was okay, and it's possible I shooed her away and kept drinking until my blurry vision turned black.

There we sat, keeled over empty shot glasses, possibly screaming at one another. Maybe the manager stopped by us because we were becoming women she didn't recognize. Women belonging hopelessly to themselves.

I had pulled the dress off falling up the stairs, laughing on our way to the dorm. I woke up the next day like I always did, with the sunrise, except this time I was in my underwear covered in fuchsia, and it struck me, she had left me this way. To my right I saw that her suitcase was gone, and a panic rose in me. I checked under my bed, scrambling for my journal only to open the shoebox and find it empty. I threw on my forest green dress, and though it was already blistering hot outside I had the need to throw on a light sweater and splash water on my face before I zipped to the front desk.

"Your friend," Marura said, glancing away from the computer, as if she knew I'd be coming. "She left with her husband after you both came from the bar."

"You mean, he came all the way from Nairobi?"

"No. He was at the hotel down the street."

"The one I always go to?"

"Yes."

Marura gave a quick wave to a group of travelers grabbing complimentary Lipton tea and mandazis before turning her attention back to me. Their chatter lowered and upon side-eyeing them I recognized that I had become that menacing tourist complaining about my woes to someone who'd rather complete her assignment on her desktop.

"She took a room here because it had gotten late. But she's always coming to the bar for a drink."

"She's a regular, here?"

"Mhmm."

She turned to smile at another traveler who took the clipboard off the reception desk to sign up for some water excursion. The scraggly man said hello to me but I could only frown. Even with the doors open and the fan going at high speed the man had managed to make the room smell like the inside of a filthy armpit. He was an easy target to loathe.

"A notebook was left for you." Her comment had come at a good moment. She opened the safe box behind the reception desk and retrieved a spiral notebook.

"Who left it?" I asked.

"She did." Marura flipped through the book and stopped at a page that had been folded at the corner with writing scrawled across it.

Places I'll visit:

The Maldives. Cambodia. South Africa. Spain. Mombasa again. Then I'll go home. He won't be there.

"But she stole," I cried.

"Sorry," she said, "but the policy states that the Sunshine Breeze Hostel is not responsible for any damaged, lost, or stolen items. Next time, please bring your valuables to our lockbox and we'll keep them safe for you at—"

"No," I shouted. "She went. No explanation. Why do that?"

Marura handed me a tissue with an unusual gentleness before saying her infamous line, but soon another guest fumbled to the front desk with a more pressing lament.

A Decision

Nigeria and the United States, late 1970s. Uduak.

They kept her close enough to watch but far enough to forget. Safely contained in the back room with the most space and all the windows, that's where they stored her. It was considered the best room in the house, but it was common knowledge it was also the most isolated. One had to walk past all the bedrooms and bathrooms to get there, and no one ever had to go that far for anything, since it was the special room kept for a special guest. Still, the old woman had more gusto than usual and managed to surprise Uduak when she said she could see Ekpewan. She had faced in their direction as they entered the room and said, "That's my baby. Our hair's the same. Thick thick o." How she was able to see her was puzzling, but it confirmed the grandma had something potentially disastrous in her DNA, which meant they all did. Soon as the mother returned to

America, her firstborn's hair would be cut and plaited until further notice.

Uduak sat by her bed, relieved that her mother had moved the old woman to the nicest room in the house, with plenty of sunlight and room for one to walk and air themselves out. She was surprised at how her mother cried when she saw that the woman who birthed her would soon die, which was another surprise, because it was obvious Grandma was satisfied even as she was marching towards her Maker. Everyone was doting on her, everyone was doing what she said, everyone was listening to the pastor she had summoned from some village she had nothing much to do with (the one who was put in the guest room upon her request) to advise her and the family on how best to handle the passing of a matriarch. The old woman was already in heaven.

She insisted on holding the child, who soon fell asleep on her sagging breasts, while she sat comfortably in the plush recliner. She had insisted she be allowed to put her feet up and lay back on the fancy chair, one of the few Western comforts she allowed herself without disparaging it. Uduak watched the two, observing they made a good pair.

"When *you* die, they'll bury you alone. No one else will go in there with you. It's not allowed. You hear?" she said. Uduak, rightly confused, second-guessed if it was her the old woman was speaking to, as she was speaking in a different tone and sounding unlike herself. "Grandma?" she asked.

"Your voice is your own. Your path is your own. Your life is your own. Mine took me from the village to this fine room. Where will yours take you?"

Grandma had beckoned her to come closer so she could touch her face, muttering that she could only see the baby and no one else. "You are making this child suffer o. Why?" she asked, suddenly. "Can't you use your voice to grow something good between you two?"

Uduak became saddened by the immediate thought that bubbled up after hearing her grandma. Let the dead bury the dead. The old woman's final intervention on her behalf would not serve anyone, certainly not her. The baby would have to make due with who her mother was, and the mother would have to brace herself for whoever this baby became. After a brief reckoning with her inner constitution, she submitted to the reality that she wouldn't be softening her temperament for the foreseeable future. She kissed the old woman on the forehead and mumbled, I love you. Perhaps she could have used her voice as a salve to heal the baby, but the fact of the matter was that she did not have it to give. It was a shock to see Grandma before she passed. Her skin, the rich color of chocolate turned ashen. That's how she knew death would come in minutes because it was like watching the color fade out. Her eyes were useless and now she used her hands to trace noses, eyes, and rub hair to sense who was there. Life had taken away the essentials from her, draining her vitality breath by breath. The only trait of hers left was her brash voice, yapping away in the room with no one paying much attention. Uduak couldn't help but think that death was the final insult.

What will the weather be today? This was the thought that initially plagued her when setting foot on American soil. On extreme occasions, there could be flooding, but most of the time the weather was pretty even. It would be hot and humid during the summer. But still. There were some details she could not quite predict and account for, like the wind. Even the American forecast, with all its pomp and circumstance, could not tell you everything that was going to happen. Back home the women knew if the weather smelled like rain or dust. But here, amidst the drawl of the South, her memory for how to know what would be coming was having its own storm. It had been foreseen that she would lose these gifts once sinking into the temperament of a new country. And she lost them because she had no intention of using them in this unfamiliar terrain. All great gifts must be used, and Uduak was perfectly happy to let these particular gifts die.

But the women she knew from home were able to see into the future. They followed the trends and made their predictions accordingly. Example: Her mother was known for her industriousness, beauty, and wisdom. Her husband adored her and the children; they listened to the words she spoke in the hopes that one day they'd be like her. While pregnant, the first baby her mother had hummed to came out with its eyes open and mouth closed. The infant wanted to see who had shored up her faith to bear the disappointment of not entering this human incarnation, releasing its last breath once laying eyes on her mother. When the newborn noted the woman's face, she felt enough ease to let go. Some years later, another baby was born. A bit wiser from its first death, this baby was ready for its human incarnation, following the mother's hum and having noted her face, she made it back into the right belly. She knew the importance of listening to this woman she chose as her mother. She would listen to every word this woman said. This was her vow and this child was Uduak, and though she'd never say it out loud, she always had a feeling that she had attempted to come into the world before and had finally gotten it right on the fourth try. How else could she describe the strange affection she had for her mother? She had a faded memory of coming in and out of one world into the next and tapping her feet while waiting in line to come in again.

"In my day, a woman's education was not worth anything. But now the day is different. It's not the time to sit at home while the man makes the money. You all better go to school," her mother had said.

She heard this statement as a warning and promised herself from then on that nothing would distract her from her studies.

That's why she considered it the ultimate distraction to have her father-in-law coming to evaluate a terrible situation that she wanted to move on from. She wondered if she should behave like those pesky weeds that disturbed her grandma when she was a child. The old woman had despised the innate stubbornness of a weed and demanded that she pluck every single one out when they'd garden. This became a point of contention between the two, as Uduak believed that if a weed grew then it had a right. It was the only fuss she ever made with any adult in her life, the right for a weed to grow, with her standing firmly as the plant's spokesman. And now it had been awhile since the old woman had gone, and all she could consider was what she would do with the life she had been given.

Upon learning the fullness of how Usen's father understood the story of her husband's disappearance, she thought of that little girl she had been, upturning her nose and refusing to do what she was told. According to her father-in-law's version of events, his son's departure from their marital bed was sudden, and the stack of unsealed letters he carried in his moleskine briefcase proved this, because that son of his never sent him one note saying he was ready to leave. How could he after all? Every letter suggested he was devoted to the union he had agreed to. Never did he write that he was going to leave.

His wife's accounting of events was that her husband had left the marriage a while ago. His coming and going was nothing sudden, more like a simmering stew about to boil. He had been a touch-and-go husband from the day he said "I do." And he had quit the marriage long before he decided to go, and you can't keep a leaving spouse, anyway. A few days before his final departure, his footsteps dragged up the stairwell and she rushed to find a broom before opening the door. She held the end of the broom towards his chest, thankful for the chain lock keeping them each on their sides. He snarled that he had bought a one-way ticket home and that she had better follow him if she didn't want to disgrace herself.

"Sure," she said with that voice she reserved solely for him. "Send the money for the ticket and I'll follow. A good husband you are." She ached to throw a lit match on him, prove to herself that she could take him, but it was best that she let him fumble down the stairs into the night. And she was lucky that he didn't slam himself against the door as he had previously done.

She was surprised to find out that he had sent letters to his father telling elaborate tales of having the highest marks in class and using his physiology textbooks as pillows to sleep in the library. Pictures of him were sent as proof of his efforts; her father-in-law showed her a picture of his son folding his arms while leaning suavely against the magnolia tree a block away from campus. The second picture she saw was the one of him grinning and shaking the hand of a stumpy white-haired professor. These were the pictures her father-in-law—Dr. Nyong—carried around to brag about his eldest boy. It was proof that he as a Big Man had raised his son to become like him.

He'd never outwardly share his glee with Usen, for he had gone through great lengths to flog any inkling for validation out of his son knowing full well that his firstborn craved this. But such a misguided craving emboldened the father to withhold tenderness from him. From early on he feared his firstborn would tarnish the family name. He knew that no amount of thrashing and pulling the ears could push the boy to sit up. So he did the next best thing when Uduak told him she had not known his whereabouts for a month. He hurled the ripped envelopes and photos on the coffee table aiming for a new target. "You are the wife," he said.

Anyone observing her would have thought she was a saint wrapped up with a dustbin of a husband, but he was sure he was not dealing with a saint. Unlike his son, who had been shielded from seeing any of the carnage from the war, he knew that she had seen the dead, and subsisted on mushrooms and snails during the fighting, and was fully aware of the war snapping at her feet. He had sensed a chill inside her, imagining a shard of ice residing in the young woman, causing her to keep love at an arm's length. He had believed that such a quality would be a necessary evil to wrangle Usen, that's what he had done after all, that's what his wife (bless her soul) had done, and this was the task his daughter-in-law should have taken up as soon as she uttered the vows, for better or for worse. From what he surmised, she had let Usen turn into Usen-the-Insane. In the village to the city this would be the moniker that followed him to the grave. His son's epithet had been written, that he could concede, but there were two players here, so what of her part?

Her father-in-law, a broad-shouldered man with thick-rimmed glasses, was respected as someone who gave the answers rather than asking the questions. It was noticed by many when he traveled to his village after graduating from a university in London. He gave the answers whether it was to a subordinate or wayward son, and for him, there was no real distinction. His delivery was like waiting for molasses to pour into a bottle. It had taken him forever and a day to say a few words to the bride and groom. But the memory of him saying, "Treat each other well," lingered in her mind. For a moment she was saddened by the way the relationship had turned out, shuddering at her apathy towards it all. The truth was, she wanted that framed degree more than anything because she had earned it, for everything that had occurred, and she wouldn't go on divulging everything for fear of crawling into bed with the baby in her arms and suffocating both of them under the blanket.

When Uduak shrugged her shoulders, signaling that she had no clue why her husband fled his own household, the father immediately relayed the content from his son's most scathing letters, naming her skinny frame as the culprit for her inability to give him a child at the beginning of their marriage. He included that she had failed to charm him, largely because she had yet to look like a woman. Hips, thighs, buttocks, waist, all of these well-known attributes were missing from her frame. And she did not do her part to play up any becoming features.

She recalled those days, when Usen skulked about the one-bedroom, visibly upset that they had no good news to send the family, and said it was her doing. When the baby was born, he pounded the door holding a disposable camera, demanding that he take a picture of them to send home. She glibly obliged, holding the screaming baby in her arms, content that his people would see she had held up her end of the bargain. Usen couldn't even see how odd his daughter was, but he did pat her on the head, even managing to hold her for a minute or so before his eyes shifted in embarrassment. His sole aim was to get the picture, and the picture he got. Her husband pulled out the Kodak, positioning her and the screaming child in front of books, demanding that she smile with her full teeth in view. She had given up her plaits for a slick Jheri curl and had grown bold in her second year as his wife. In defiance she asked, "What pictures have you seen Nigerians smile in?" Not the passport photo. Not the family photo. Not the school photo. Not the work ID. Not ever. She closed her mouth and glared at the camera.

She didn't know that when the picture and copy of the birth certificate was received his father had planned to fly into Houston at the end of the month.

She learned that he had a separate p.o. box where she couldn't interfere with his messages. But Dr. Nyong saw that Uduak was not the intercepting kind, which signaled to him that she must have quietly endured their marriage while finding salvation in her studies and Christ.

Records of Fela, the Jackson 5, Chaka Khan, Ray Charles, and every Motown band one could name were lined up alphabetically, with empty two-dollar-whiskey bottles holding pens and pencils on his desk. This was a trait in Usen that baffled the father, the level of organization his son could maintain in his dishevelment. Maybe that was a talent in and of itself.

He rose from the loveseat to peruse the apartment, leaning over with his hands behind his back to peer closer at artifacts as if it were a museum. He wiped his handkerchief across his forehead, saying, "You'll come with me."

"Why?" she asked.

"The scenario you're in is no good."

"Hmm."

"You drove him away."

"No, sir."

"How could he just go, then?"

"Why does anyone just go?" she said, forgetting herself. "They go because they can."

He saw a stain on the arm of the chair and assessed that it would have been better had they bought a leather couch, which they could have afforded because money was Western Unioned for furnishings.

"You made a comfortable home for him?"

"I tried."

"Tried?"

"I studied, sir. I was focused. What else?"

He had initially thought his daughter-in-law had a personality that appreciated the importance of heeding the advice of those who knew more than she did. If he had to tell her father anything, it would be that the girl had grown into someone who thought first of herself and second about others. Having realized this truth, he didn't care to prolong the conversation any further. "Let's settle this as Africans," he said. "That is who we are, no? It is a grave disappointment that you both have adopted the mistakes of American living; the most fatal is the poisonous idea that one can go it alone."

"And my studies?"

"My dear, your responsibilities are as follows: Wife first, mother second, and school when the former two items are expertly achieved."

She excused herself to the kitchen to make tea.

"Would you like honey or sugar, sir?" she hoped her voice had carried into the living room.

He let out a short, "ah-ah!" expressing his surprise that she didn't bring both on the tray as her mother had always done. The women of her tribe were excellent caretakers, which is what his son needed and what her mother should have taught her to provide. "Sugar," he replied.

156

Uduak teetered in the kitchen wondering what secrets to tell him in exchange for her staying in the country. He'd never drag her away, but this was about optics and she had to be careful. She was now a *been to*, someone who had been to a place and would now be known by the people that had followed her and left her. To smooth out the damage that had already occurred, she was ready to give collateral. But what? A terrible secret, a secret she had hoped to take to her grave could be the information that granted her immunity. When Usen consumed all the liquor his tummy could hold, and it was just the two of them alone, he threw furniture and books against the wall. She would leave it there and let the-father-in-law's imagination fill in the bits. No one would blame her for wanting to put an ocean between her and a man like that. She could allow the message that she was afraid for her life to spread far and wide, but would this be enough? He had been flinging her about for the better part of the year, and after she was flung, well, she went back to reading her books. This tidbit, she'd keep to herself.

As she rummaged for the sugar, she considered that anything involving Usen would identify her as a culprit because she had attended both the native and white wedding where she uttered the words, "Let nothing tear what God has put together." Best to work another angle. Making a case about the ghosts that changed the color of any white-picketed-fence dream she had could be a strategic move. With all she had experienced so far, attaining her degree would give substance to her trouble, as an immigrant, as a foreigner. Soon as she arrived there were so many boxes to tick and labels to accept; Christian, Ibibio, and a woman was not enough to manage in a new land. She had been humiliated simply for being herself. How fair was that? To have to argue with people who think the way God made you isn't right?

There were ghosts that spooked her in the night. Ones she had never met, though they seemed familiar.

In secondary school, her teacher had spanked any student who could not recite the rivers that ran through all the states in the US. She wanted to see the Rio Grande when her teacher called it the lifeline of Texas and said Americans vacationed every month with excursions to photograph such attractions. But then it was these phantoms who were the first to greet her when she arrived, and no one cared to tell her about this, that she was entering a haunted country. The creatures crept into her slumber, showing her scenes of people throwing themselves into the river and holding their breath whenever they stood on soil. Wasn't this a shame considering all the well wishes she had received saying her life should have been blessed?

"My dear, be coming," he called.

Her baby, who by now could sleep through any argument or thunderstorm, began sobbing and she was sure to sob in her usual staccato spurts if she didn't soon go to meet her. But it was those cries that struck a wild idea in her.

Perhaps Nigeria wasn't home anymore, but for the child, it could be. She'd grow up with her mother tongue before turning into someone else. There was still time for the child, for Ekpewan, to receive more favor than she had. The baby's voice went higher resting on a nasally cry. Her mother went into the tiny living room—forgetting the tea—with her hands akimbo.

"Sir, this is how I'm seeing things . . ."

A week later, she had sent the child home with her father-in-law for goodwill. It was a gesture that acknowledged the gravity of the matter as a baby's life swung between two worlds. What mother would throw her child away and not come back? Soon as the diploma touched her palm, she'd be on the first flight home. *Three years*, she had pleaded. *Three.* The father-in-law was hesitant but after an hour of drinking tea and biscuits he reluctantly agreed.

Uduak's mother, upon hearing the news, said, "Ah! You would have told me about this, now. You know how he is. Usen. He will hold that child to control you and don't you see that by controlling you he will now control us, and all this because you would rather trade in your motherhood to stay in a foreign country, Jesus. My dear, we are all in for a ride." Her mother could not say much more as she had seen the picture of Uduak's new hairstyle which clued her in to the fact that the girl had grown some. The mother understood her daughter's stance, though she'd never tell her that if she had been thrust into similar circumstances, she'd have done more of what she had always wanted to do. But she couldn't allow herself to focus entirely on Uduak's predicament because it was now a predicament for all. As she considered the situation with a bird's-eye view, the mother was compelled to hear the thing you cannot hear, and see the thing you cannot see, and revealed a premonition to her daughter.

"Na wow o. You have sent that child to die."

Plot 196

Nigeria, 2020. Arit.

I'll never be that kind of woman to you. That's what I told him. The first time we met there was no touching of any sort. We were aware that something deadly was going around and it wasn't the flu. We kept our distance. "I'm Igala," he said. "Do you know what tribe that is?" He half-smiled, like he had guessed something about me and it turned out right. I had never heard of this tribe before, and there'd be many more to know after this encounter. But never mind all that. Since he introduced himself this way I've forgotten his first name, so I call him Mr. Igala, not to his face of course, because that would hurt him. He had that look in his eye—you've seen that look I'm sure—that impossible look a man gives when he wants to plaster his yearning over a woman.

He said, "I'm just loving you."

And with no smile or frown I said, "That's nice."

He wanted an answer. Men always need answers when they keep praying you'll come around and become their lawfully wedded ball and chain. It's like they think their prayer is more righteous than your right to be free.

"No rush," he said. "One day you'll be fixing me a nice soup and be the first one to praise in the worship hall."

But I told him. I've moved to Plot 196, two streets from the bypass near Christ Lives Church on a road where a family of chickens, freaky deaky barefoot children with begging bowls, and a mai-ruwa* walk by.

He don't know why it's got to be this way, but you do, and she does, and you know I've never cut in a straight line. I packed up a duplex with running water, twenty-four-hour electricity, and a crystal shop on the corner to move to a place with no street sign. A place where if you give directions to the okada driver who's delivering your veggie-no-sweetcorn-please pizza he'll say he'll get there in a few minutes. An hour later you'll call, where are you, you'll say, you'll give more descriptors to explain where you live. *When you reach Christ Lives Church, take an immediate turn by the booth where a lady sells data, chin-chin, malt, and then turn immediately to your left on an unpaved road. Three houses down to your right that's where I live, you get? It's the rusty gate with the poster of pastor John (I forget his last name but it starts with an O), you'll see mai guard in front, he's wearing a red cap, and he'll let you through.*

*Term for water cart pusher

162

Please be attentive as you can't miss pastor John and Festus staring at you if you're on the right street.

He'll say he can't find it, that he passed by Christ Lives Church and didn't see you there, and you bite your lip because you thought you had made it obvious in your enunciated English that you were in fact, at home. You'll send him your live location (but he don't have a smartphone so that won't work), and then you'll try having him meet you by the place where those guys sit in lawn chairs selling petrol (an easy enough landmark to spot but we all know *that* won't work). He won't get it though—*ma I cannot find you*—and so you say you'll meet him at the church in five minutes and he says, yes ma, I'll be there, and when ten minutes have gone you realize, this man is lost. So you call and you say, where are you?, and he says, Oh, sorry ma, I'm not seeing the church nau, this road is confusing o . . . and then naturally your only logical recourse is to scream for your motherfuckin' life.

Your screaming gets him to where he needs to be in less than five minutes, to that place where those guys sitting in the plastic white chairs sell petrol. You find that it's not your attempt to give clear directions in a calm manner that worked, but it's your ability to yell in the middle of a dusty road that gets him to understand you. And so he removes the veggie-no-sweetcorn-please pizza from a dilapidated tote bag, and the pizza box is cold and the cheese looks like rubber. An appropriate quarantine meal for a woman who fled America to live on Plot 196.

To make peace with a street you don't particularly like but every day you must wake to greet it, that's the dance I'm in these days. And I got folks crowding in, vying for attention because it's a lockdown and there's nothing much to do but dial the person you love.

She sends letters, you know? Since I fled away I get emails from Nkechiexplainsitall@gmail.com. Every week on Fridays around 11 p.m. PST, which is Saturday morning my time, the subject header reads, *Hey Sis*. 11 p.m. has always been the hour her night of debauchery begins, puffing Mary J and blasting Afro-pop videos from *YouTube*, for nostalgia's sake. She'll puff herself into the "chill zone" and catch inspiration there. I'd often tap out of the whole trip by twelve or one, being that I was grasping at straws for a restful sleep and she could stay on the high well into the morning. She writes:

Hey Sis,

Do you know you took my dream with you when you packed yourself away? I always wanted to go back, I was born there after all, schooled in Lagos, speak pidgin, speak it better than you, know three languages and that's more my home than yours anyway, not trying to be mean but I was born there and you weren't. Just saying. You snuck out and packed a suitcase with my dream in tow. Broke my heart. And what a parting gift you gave, the gift of your bare behind out for the world to see. Sis, what a way to go. I'm

164

lucky I found you that day. You said you were going to eat and I knew you'd be there, so I went after you. Don't you know you ran down one of the scariest streets in Oakland. Fool. They grab girls that look like us to move from this city to that, for you-know-what, and here you were running up the block bare-ass naked. Well, why didn't you tell me you wanted to streak that day? You're my friend, if you needed to blow off steam I would have streaked with you. For solidarity's sake. You know I don't mind that sort of thing. I'm your friend.

I found you, tits and ass and barefoot and you know, I almost admired you. Never thought you'd take it so far but I saw you could go further than me and a part of me wanted to clap and another wanted to pretend I didn't know you. But when I saw you turning to go up the hill, I tailed you, told the driver, "Follow that car," and he said, "What do you think this is? Get out." And I thought—if this were Nigeria and I paid him enough money, he'd have done it.

When the police arrived, I thought I'd jump in, but they held you down and a man put his arm between me and you and said, "Stand back," and that was the first time I ever felt fear in this country. I realized that for some of us it's been easy to live, but for most of us, it's been hard. I actually prayed that night (I guess you might call it prayer? Anyway, I tried speaking to God, after smoking of course). I prayed that I'd never end up on a scary street shouting about what someone did in my mother's house. Don't think you even remember that part. but you kept screaming that you tried to tell

165

*her what happened. On God. You swore it. You said
since you weren't sure it was safe to swear on your
mother you'd swear on God. That's why I called her.
She needed to see this side of you. Buy the ticket. Take
that flight. See you. I didn't mean to betray you. But
your Mom says you never told her anything about
what happened. She said she didn't know. She even
cried. Well not entirely, her eyes looked like they would
drop tears but they never dropped. And I could tell
she's not the type to do that, to show the side of her
that wants to cry. I don't know what to believe, sis, but
I was left shook. You took my confidence with you, you
get that? I used to worry about your death but now I
worry about mine. But thanks for sending me a text
telling me you're alright. Clearly, I miss you.*

*So how's it there? How's working remotely? How
you handling the Rona? You're social distancing,
right? Well, you definitely are social distancing because you've been distancing yourself from me for like
what, two years now? Did I hurt you, somehow? Tell
me, you can tell me, I'm your friend, remember? The
one you met in Phaustine's Island where I found you
eating okra soup with your tears dripping into the
bowl? It bugged me that you were eating that way,
and I let you know. Then you sniffled, "Mind your
business" and the rest was gravy.*

*When you're up to it, let me know if you're good,
and if you're good, then I'll send back a text saying,
please remember that you are loved and you packed
my dreams with you. If you're not I'll send a text saying I'm sorry.*

Nkechi

P.S.

Have you fallen in love yet? Probably not...you're so skittish with love.

Mr. Igala made a life as an administrator in the North, you know? Got his start in Jos, then lived in Benue for a hot second and ended up in Abuja working as an advisor to some Big Man who makes Big Money. He has a house in Maitama and wants a wife living there in a year. Thinks 'cause I laid down with him a few times I'mma come up a wife. Says, *I'll take you everywhere, first stop to my village where they make good draw soup from the bark of a tree.* We met before the restaurants and bars closed. He asked for a date having met me at a soirée where expats and locals mingled.

At the the ultra-fancy-schmoozy-shindig we snatched our chairs from the dining hall and made a circle in the courtyard to discuss Berger roundabout, the rough-and-tumble junction where the routes of governors, criminals, soothsayers, sellers, night girls, children, and people of every religious persuasion converge in the heavily trafficked area, where the big shot could swerve into the boy selling paintings and for a moment they are both trapped in the same dread. A young artist spoke of her encounter with the supernatural while she was coming from a long-time client's house. She did hair and nails for a living and made extra money from home service work. It was at the roundabout where she said a man brought a pot of egusi soup as big as three average-sized people. He boasted to the onlookers that he could eat the pot in five minutes if someone cooked him some nice pounded yam. Someone brought him the pounded yam, a pot as big as one average-sized person, and the people waited for the man with a pot of soup the size of three people to eat up. He bent over the two pots and in a minute the pots were empty. She could vouch on her child that it was empty because she had peered inside the pot herself. Staging an illusion that quickly was not very plausible, which dumbfounded the onlookers. Being that it was dusk moving into darkness he could have manipulated their sight, but one hundred people's eyes never let their eyes off him.

They mumbled, "How?" But then again, she rationalized, it was dusk turning to night and Nigerians are smart in their cleverness to stage the impossible. This wasn't her biggest concern, however, finding her way home was her biggest preoccupation that evening. Her one chance to get home couldn't be her last chance and robberies were high as of late. Because if a knife was pulled out in the car and she had to empty her pockets, that was it. Her things would never be recovered because, as everyone in the circle agreed, nothing ever works in Nigeria.

In the circle of the like-minded I had met, Mr. Igala, who began his monologue by quoting 1

Corinthians 13. "Some of you are too intellectual for church and have given into atheism, but I remain a man of God," he said, "and I'm ashamed of this country because we do not bear with each other in love the way Christ did. If a woman is selling a bushel of oranges at 500 naira, I guarantee that someone will negotiate down the price and scoff, 'Why not 300?' Doesn't he care that this woman needs her 500 to feed? That is this country. We are a land where love is lost."

In response I snapped my fingers in agreement and said, "The loss isn't only in this country. It's dispersed across the globe, wherever our parents went and raised us, that loss has traveled abroad."

Later he caught me nibbling on a samosa with delicious chili-lime sauce and said, "I'm impressed." My curiosity was piqued and thus our story began.

Whenever he talks about him and I, he says, we. *We*. We'll figure it out, we'll handle it, we'll fix it. "Why you rather swat insects than live with me?" he whines. "You should've come to my place. The guest wing you could have had."

But oh, how I feel the tug of a cord forming between us if I allow myself to live in the house he pays for. "This is about us," he says, reminding me of the great scare of the virus separating Nigerians from everyone else. "Your American friends evacuated and the ones who stayed don't call you, and soon you'll have to concede that you're one of us." He cracks mid-sentence, Mr. Igala, losing the official nature that usually defines his timbre. Of him, he

169

has two presiding qualities, he's certain about his certainty and is notorious for staying within the given bounds. A stiff collar he wears crisp and rigid.

Informing him of my life before Plot 196, a life of dousing myself in pixie dust and watching my best friend slapping random folks with a paddle would insult him. I answer him the only way I can, "I choose this country."

And can't two people sleep together and stay friendly without that overbearing sense of ownership? He has the gall to behave like our exchange is a mutual benefit, and yes, he gives what he can, but then again if having a dip in my body is the exchange that'll quell his irritations, then it's apparent that I have given much more.

He sees it's a hard time for me living on this plot, an American girl without an A/C or a working generator to charge all her American shit. A pile of trash sits outside my gate and a procession of cows leave hunks of poo along the road and I worry that if I'm not careful I'll become like Plot 196. Rough and wild with ditches swallowing those in her way whole. But I sleep well here. Lay on my mattress in the nude pressing my sweat against the surface and let the breeze of the fan hit me all over.

The flower bushes on Plot 196—the ones next to the dumpster—they're not soft or fragrant. They look like dagger petals; I pricked a finger when I grabbed a bunch to put in a jar, and I couldn't tell if I was smelling the waste boiling in the sun or the flower. Can't tell one smell from the other 'cause the entire road's too funky. A mix of waste, jollof, odorless flowers, and something burning with dust kicking up in your face.

And the street children that play on the road are funky too, funky like accidentally drinking past-due milk. In front of the compound, one girl, no older than six, was sucking off a boy, no older than eight, hiding behind no bush, no building, no dumpster, but stood in front of Plot 196, in front of pastor John, a tableau of a girl crouching to slurp a boy's wee-wee, while he ate from a bag of potato chips. They could have gone somewhere discreet, found a hallway in one of those abandoned buildings, gone behind a pile of wood and rot where no one would see them, or better yet, do what they were doing in the dark. But they didn't seem to know the difference between day and night, proper and improper, and if they were already this bold, they wouldn't care much for the pleas of a foreigner. It was wise not to speak and reveal this fact to them. I yelped. A trail of saliva cum stuck to the girl's bottom lip as she turned away from this boy's thumb-sized penis. The boy zipped his pants, continued walking and never looked back, while the girl walked forward craning her neck to watch my astonishment while my throat cinched tight.

But I won't knock Plot 196. Who am I to knock anything in this country? Still haven't forgotten two

months prior going on a hike with friends and meeting twenty or so teenagers smoking by the waterfall
in the forest. We had the bright idea to trek to the
outskirts of town where the roads get dustier and
more unpaved as you go. We went in with iPhones,
Androids, a shiny speaker, government IDs, bank
cards, and not much common sense. We climbed uphill, past the empty glass bottles that had been
thrown in the water. I was even so bold to wear a
halter that day. They found us deep in the forest,
bringing daggers, machetes, a shovel, and a cutlass.
They threw a rock and raised a shovel, and took our
money and gadgets. This area is insecure, the towns-
folk said. People limp out of the bush sobbing over
all manner of attacks, stabbings, muggings, rapes,
death, and you go in there with four men and three
women thinking what? Good thing they didn't hurt
you, good thing they didn't take you, good thing you
got to run. You'll raise the money to replace the lost
items and pay the motivation fee so the police will
file the necessary reports because this is Nigeria, and
anything you want you will simply have to pay. Next
time, go in there with twenty escorts, and tell those
twenty escorts to carry twenty guns, and then you
may take pictures under the waterfall.

But back to Mr. Igala. The one requesting an "I'll
fix you a nice soup" wife. He enjoys a version of me
that I'll soon give up to make it here. Seems like the
only way to rise in anything is to let yourself die in
the face of it.

Another Woman Leaves Home

Nigeria, 2020. Faith.

She had been praying for a miracle like women in her predicament do. With not much money in her pocket, and that recent memory of her senior sister kicking her out because an extra mouth to feed was too much on a household with three children and a grumpy husband, she was low. She would have grieved her lot—the constant sting of being a burden to those around you, having to spend your money before you could save it, and having very little to build a suitable life for yourself—but she had been taught that showing disbelief in the face of a challenge was unbecoming of a believer. She had just finished hearing a sermon on the book of Job at a home service. Who could say how God was preparing to bless and shower his favor upon her? Still, she had an itch that needed scratching and a mild discontent that chipped away at her serenity when assessing her circumstances. It wasn't like a gash in need of immediate attention, but it pestered her enough that she knew living with such discontent would only lead to a more complex wound down the road. She traded in her frustrations for a desire that life would one day yield to her. The salve would reveal itself soon she hoped, and in the meantime, she'd bear with the itch and exercise some patience.

If she woke up every day with that mysterious ability to fill her body with air, an achievement she had absolutely nothing to do with, then a force beyond her must have regarded her well enough to let her live. She only wished this power from beyond could turn Himself into a person with flesh, bones, blood, a heart, and strong arms to hold her and say, I love you.

If her life had little prospect of getting better, then she hoped that things didn't get any worse. When she had lived further north, it was the farm life, until her sister married and she soon followed her to J-town. The city was better than Kaduna, with more possibilities to make a living, but then she found herself questioning everything about the new place. Of all the things that bothered her, it was that most of the honey sold in the markets was no good. It was too thick and lacked a certain glisten to it, looking weighed down and browner than she liked. She knew exactly what the seller would say after she'd declare—*you all mixed this honey?* The vendor would give a pitiful reply, perfectly content to sell a fake product for a few kobos. "This honey is fresh o. I tell you no lie, ma." But she knew better than to believe *that,* and stood akimbo waving her claw-like hands in front of the seller's nose. *If the ants come racing when the honey drips that means you cooked with sugar. You think I don't know honey?* She knew bees, she saw upfront how the gooey nectar was made. In this place someone could tell you a shirt was green even if it was yellow, so long as they made the naira they needed. *You disgrace yourself.*

Liars. All of them. Most of them. That's what she concluded. And the only way to catch a liar peddling fake liquid gold was to start a good business of her own, because what would people do if they didn't realize a seller with a 419* spirit, or were too stressed in their lives to harp on another problem? They'd never get a chance to taste a sweet that had never been tampered with. Her banner (when she could afford one) would read like this:

"Faith's Natural Honey."

Hers would be real, not like what others would do where they'd rip the legs of bees and slice their wings in a bottle to pass it off as natural. On her next trip to the village she'd take the empty plastic water bottles she collected and fill them. Charge 2000 naira each and let her customers taste for them-selves. She made this her business for a year or two as she cobbled some odd jobs together. She was thankful that the little she had was able to stop her from trekking further south with those other dis-placed women—her contemporaries—who had less options than she did.

*A scam

These women would bring their children down to some kind of city, staying outdoors on some kind of street, where they and their children begged for some kind of scrap, or where they hawked some kind of produce, or some kind of appliance, or even worse, hawked their very own bodies And something happens to someone when they realize their body has now been factored into the category of a mere sum. Anyone with a pulse understands that selling yourself on a street where you must beg and hawk has to take something away from you. You may not know what that something is, and you may even feel that you wield a type of power because you get to select who your buyer is, but you know full well that if there was another possibility then most likely you'd take that. And it's at that moment when these women who find themselves on a busy street realize the thing they're selling is not a random something, it is everything. And how does one cope with giving everything to someone who may see you as a meaningless thump behind a bush?

Faith wondered if women like this could even pray, and immediately thanked God for not giving her the life of a woman who had to make this kind of choice. For women who made these kinds of choices were not entirely welcomed in her church, unless they repented and fixed themselves to become someone else, of course.

Up until her departure from her elder sister's compound, she was happy to have four walls, a roof, a duvet and a pillow on the floor. She slept on a rug in her nieces' and nephew's room. If she slept with a second pillow she could cope, avoiding soreness in her neck. She knew that her presence stressed the family. When they had their prayers, she'd quietly excuse herself to read her Bible. When they'd fast, she'd eat outside. When they went to the Mosque, she went somewhere else, although she didn't have to, it seemed better to appear to have a place to go. "Why convert?" her sister asked one day. "Are you not one of us?"

During the lockdown, her brother-in-law started to watch the food going in and the food going out, and he noted whose mouth the food was going into. They had to start feeding once a day to ration the portions. Her sister's clients had stopped calling since everyone was now cooking at home and looking to save money. Her husband, a taxi driver, had to deal with long fuel queues, less customers, and frequent police stops checking to see if he was following the two-riders-per-car rule. And the days when he couldn't work and stayed home with his wife, a daughter, another daughter, a son, and *her*, well . . . why? *Why didn't she find herself a marriage so her husband could take over?* He had never signed up to have two wives and get half the benefit. That's what he'd tell his wife behind their bedroom door, but with everyone in close quarters his words and exasperation reached every nook.

When Faith was on the bus to Abuja, she was thankful for the fancy jacket she wore that would carry her to her next life. She had phoned a distant cousin who knew of a churchgoing family looking for a house girl. They agreed for her to stay on the floor of this cousin's flat for a week and then—God willing—live with the family looking to employ a staff. Yet, she was disenchanted with the thought of working for another family who could grow tired of her for reasons she couldn't control. If she broke a glass it could be nicked from her salary and her mistake could be used against her, and since her hands trembled when she was around company that made her anxious, she knew she'd break a glass or two and have to prostrate herself and say, sorry. It wasn't that interesting to keep bowing and apologizing in a place where bowing and apologizing never stopped them from making a fool of you. And again, that itch she had, that itch that said she had better be careful before a woman like her actually becomes sorry. That sorry spirit was something that could take over the soul, make one dreary.

The answer to rising above her conundrum evaded her, and so she focused her mind on the nice lady who had sent her off in style. It wasn't simply that she had something nice to wear, it was that the person who gave her the jacket had also given her a nice sensation, uplifting her out of a world where kindness was a rarity. The jacket was tight at her shoulders, but she intended to wear it as much as life would allow because it was the nicest thing she owned. She spent the ride thanking God for allowing her a bit of vanity to dwell on a nice feeling for the long ride. It offset the disparaging comments of her sister saying, *you better find your marriage, sha. It's not like you're going to ever study the book.*

The gift was given to her by a woman she had met at the bank. She was there to put 15,000 naira in her account. A month's salary. Her Madam needed someone to come in every day to do the usual— wash dishes and wipe toilets. Ten hours a day for 15,000 naira a month. She wasn't even allowed to stay in the girls' quarters as her employer was wary of any scenario involving a female house help bending over to wipe a counter with the wandering eye of her husband. If the job had covered her boarding, the paltry sum would have made sense, but she knew that her boss was simply wicked. When she attempted to stop her mind from condemning the woman, she settled on this for a prayer: "God will beat you for me. He will. He will punish you for the way you are, trust me, He will. Stupid woman. You are sick in the head. You are . . ."

While she was in the queue ruminating on the many ways her evil Madam would receive due punishment, she noticed a fine woman enter the bank. The woman wore a translucent black head wrap with shiny gemstones at the end. She was heavily perfumed and Faith could smell the musk scent from behind her.

The woman in the headwrap scratched her head and let out a "Goodness!" The queue was far too long and she had little time to spare. If she were willing to grease some palms to jump the line she could have done that. She had a good excuse, her favorite daughter was coming back from university and she had to fix her a good soup. Anyone could empathize with a mother rushing to meet a child and she knew a teller—Murtala—who usually helped her husband send large transfers. He would have done what she asked without hesitation, even jumped at the chance to help her. But could you really call it help if you had to slip someone 1,000 to motivate them to get the job done? The woman— Hameeda—didn't want to compromise this part of herself. Too many compromises and soon she'd forget the line that marks right from wrong. Boundaries, especially in a place that seemed to lack them entirely, were essential. But she couldn't stand how the righteous were always left in the dust while others strong-armed and paid fees to muscle to the front. She checked her phone for the time.

In a situation like this, there was not much one could do but use the one power they had at their disposal. Complain. Suck your teeth. Stamp your feet. Crack a satirical joke, or curse someone out. And if you couldn't curse someone out then you could curse your country out. It's the only thing to do in lieu of crying. To save face, you must let at least five people know you don't like what's going on. So that's what Hameeda did, and that's how she met the lady in front of her. The third person she complained to.

"These people are not serious," she said, "not serious at all."

The lady in front of her mentioned the white tent outside with people shifting about in chairs waiting for the security to let them in the bank. Maybe that was her way of counting a blessing and noting that they were lucky to be inside.

As the queue inched forward, Hameeda observed the lady in front of her. Her nose, from the periphery, reminded her of a beak. But the shape of her nose didn't faze her too much, though it was an odd sight. It was the shape of her body that really left an impression. Too skinny, she decided. But it was possible the lady was just built that way. In this country, you could never truly know if it was the work of mild starvation or God simply bestowing one with a small frame. She decided to go with the latter as it was a more pleasant thought to settle on. *She has the frame of my firstborn, Zainab. And who knows if I'll meet her in time with the queue being the way it is?* Hameeda was almost ready to settle on defeat as her mundane observations had brought her back to her initial irritation. But then she grew hopeful as she observed the lady in front of her. If the lady was responsive to her droning, maybe she would have concern for her dilemma.

She touched her shoulder and quickly explained, "Please, I still need to go to the market to get what I need for a kuka soup for my daughter . . ."

The bird-like lady stepped to the side and said, "No problem." It was then Hameeda learned the creature's name was Faith.

A bank teller opened his desk to take customers and within a half hour Hameeda was able to make her transfer. But then she noticed the lady who had helped speed up her day and decided to not leave so quickly. She had already waited so long, and she knew if she told her favorite daughter that her soup wasn't ready because she had spent her day suffering the Nigerian factor*, the favorite daughter would understand. Even offer a word or two of consolation. That's why this daughter was undeniably her favorite.

Twenty minutes later, Faith came out, neither smiling or frowning, bracing herself to cross the street to find a taxi.

"Excuse me!" Hameeda called motioning from the window. She watched how the lady stopped in her flight when hearing her, zipping back through the crowd and remaining upright on her way to the car park.

Hameeda pulled a dark orange jacket from a nylon. "It was for my first girl, but you're about her size and the blazer gives a sophisticated look. You know, posh posh."

Faith tried it on, over her dress.

"Thank you, ma."

And then Hameeda guessed, a lady like this must need work. Her house staff—two girls about fourteen and sixteen—were not getting along. One had

*A popular expression many Nigerians use to express all the wahala they must deal with living in the country

182

wanted to sleep instead of work and the elder of the two beat her, which caused the younger house help to eat all the rice in the fridge. The elder girl knew English better than the younger one who didn't speak a word, other than saying, yes ma, yes sir, no ma, no sir, that sort of thing. The lady was older than the two and could sort them out. Or better yet, she'd send away the younger house help and replace her with . . . what was her name again?

She wanted to say a few phrases to draw them closer together but decided to leave well alone. The lady was smiling but it was hard to tell if she truly preferred to smile or if it was done because it was an acceptable reaction to an acceptable gift. Though the lady possessed a fair heart and had her daughter's frame, Hameeda assessed she was adrift somehow. To bet on a person at a loss for themselves, well, that would be a stress, and in her beloved country, she didn't want to take on another headache. She thanked the lady for her support, and ordered the driver to hurry to the market.

That night, Faith added her unlikely patron from the bank to her prayers, thanking the Lord for her generosity and asking that her heart be led to Jesus, the one who worshipped the one true God, because it was clear that the good woman was praying to the wrong one. The way she smiled to herself immediately put all the important people in her life on alert. Her elder sister accused her of wasting her salary. Her Madam grew suspicious, wondering how she could afford such a luxury, and since she was suspicious of every domestic cleaning her house, she took the blazer as a bad omen.

Two months later, Faith was fired for breaking a teacup. She had heard the length of her boss's tongue that day. Six months of her salary would not cover the cost of the cup. That's what she was told. When she searched the depths of her heart to muster an apology, nothing was there. More shocking was that she had no will to beg for her job. And that's what the Madam had wanted, she wanted this nobody to cry for the scrap that only she could give. Since her subordinate didn't grovel, it was time to find the next lowly person. A few days after, her elder sister said she had to leave her husband's house, relaying a year's worth of grievances—you don't contribute enough, you lost your job, and here you have this blazer that you clearly don't deserve, go find your way, please, you are stressing my life.

She used some money she saved and the money her sister gave her out of guilt to pay for transit to head further South, hoping she'd find favor elsewhere. She continued praying for God to change Hameeda's heart and for that very same God to seek vengeance on the lousy woman she had worked for.

"Your jacket," Mrs. Bamidele said. She had sat next to her during the church service and immediately liked her. "You're looking spiky."

Faith showed her full teeth and dimples. "Thank you, ma."

They had danced in the aisles during the entire service because the pastor kept catching the spirit and ordering the church band to play music. After the worship, a conversation began.

"I left my senior sister's place," Faith told her.

"She has a husband and children?"

"Yes, ma."

"Well then obviously you can't live there. You can only know your sister as a sister, but when she becomes a wife she is something different. She must care for her children and husband first."

"Yes, ma."

"It's good that you're making your own life. It's a must, sweetie."

"Yes, ma."

"Now see here," Mrs. Bamidele leaned in.

Faith could smell her perfume, it was like a flower but she couldn't tell what flower exactly, so she wondered if it was a foreign scent, a scent that would be unlikely to come from anywhere she'd been.

"There's this doctor who has purchased a building for a guesthouse. Say you work there? It's in a nice estate and he'd give you a room in the boys' quarters. It's much better than these jagga jagga places on the outskirts that aren't very safe for a woman alone. You'll pay 50,000 naira for the year, but you'll always have to mind your skirt. You're fairly well spoken and could help manage the needs of any guest, abi?"

"Yes, ma. Thank you, ma. God bless you, ma."

"And you have a strong voice. Rough with authority. Not very soft. That's okay though. We make use of the weaknesses we're given until it becomes our strength. People will listen to you, sha. That's all it means."

"Yes, ma."

"And you're unassuming. In a good way. Not so pretty that you'll think you can chase one of the guests for your meal ticket. You'll do an honest day's work." Mrs. Bamidele laughed, using a white napkin to dab the sweat from her forehead. "I mean no harm by this statement; really, this whole pretty nonsense is for foolish girls who end up nowhere fast. You get?"

Faith understood that her outward appearance was not what most would prefer. No man had ever asked her on a proper date, and usually people walked up to her expecting her to fetch this or fetch that, assuming that she was forever available to fetch. The truth of not having the most remarkable face had brought sadness once, because she didn't seem to have any options of a life that would involve another loving her. But these days she accepted the fact that she was still alive and would have to get her enjoyment in one way or the other. Possibly, her enjoyment would not have many people around to dote on her. But a biscuit with tea after morning service might be a shot at fulfillment. She nodded in Mrs. Bamidele's direction answering, "Yes, ma. I get."

It was settled. She would see the doctor in a week and her eccentric friend was certain she'd soon have a job. "He wants to set up his operations before he goes back abroad to teach. Let him see that you can help his efforts."

Faith lingered around after the churchgoers trickled out. A melancholy sank in as she watched everyone take their noise and gregariousness with them. What awaited her was another floor in a distant relative's home. She could ask to sleep on the floor in the praise hall. Somewhere in the back, were a dozen or so rooms with beds. She was attending one of the largest worship centers in the city, with chapters in twenty Nigerian states and in places like Bolivia and the United Kingdom. The itch that she had hoped to leave when she left, the one that had poked her in every instance until she got the gift that made her grin, was now morphing into a pain. She couldn't help but think that people are fickle. One day they'll shine their light on you, but their affection is largely fleeting and gone on a whim. In a second, they'll throw you away thinking you're the garbage they should have put out. To load oneself with the hope that people will do better has to be a sin, this she concluded. Didn't her sister once vow to take care of her only to send her away in anger? Didn't the woman from the bank leave her in the lot as soon as their business finished? And her new friend, the boisterous elder woman, was nice, but till when?

187

So let's put them in the corner, she thought. Where man disappoints, He steps in. Is it not He who takes the pitiless seeker in search of a direction and steers him closer to His vision? Why take this very church, a palace in a poor country, she thought.

That night she prayed on behalf of her new friend's soul, concluding that the elder woman could not be truly saved if she was dividing her belief between two Gods. During their conversation, the eccentric had let it slip that she rolled out a prayer mat to converse with Allah, though she said she preferred the bible. Although Faith had dropped one God for another, she'd never dare to worship two. She'd be grateful for her new friend but remain watchful.

She had accompanied Mrs. Bamidele with her entourage to the guesthouse, soon learning that her new mate rarely traveled without company. The men wore their natives, the women wore dresses with headwraps and she wore a skirt and the blazer. The doctor—a man with short fingernails and pointy ears—welcomed them to the sitting room as they immediately discussed a candidate running for governor and their hope to back him. If this man got elected, he'd remember their good deeds and help them solidify a contract . . . on the gisting went. Naturally, the guests wanted to eat as it was right after breakfast and just before lunch.

"Faith . . ." Mrs. Bamidele said, turning to half wave a finger in her direction. It was obvious that the newcomer had nothing to do with these people's business; she looked at the doctor who motioned at the door behind her and said, "In the kitchen."

When she got in there, she shuffled around the cupboards and took out trays for the bottled water, bananas, groundnuts, juice, and shortbread biscuits. By the time she served the last plate someone said, "Doctor abeg, we don already chop this small thing o. Where is your wife, now? So she may help you meet the requirements of having guests."

The doctor said that he had just bought all the ingredients he would need for soup and there was plenty to go around. Meat, kpomo, tripe, and dried fish for a substantial ogbono soup, if only someone would cook it

"That's perfect." Mrs. Bamidele said above the fray. "You bought and someone must make. Faith . . ."

Up the girl went to cook soup and turn semo while fading to the background.

"What do you think of the girl?" Mrs. Bamidele whispered, capitalizing on her absence.

"Who?" Asked the doctor.

"The woman in your kitchen."

The doctor, a man who felt he was much better with his scalpel, was sparse with his words about most subjects unrelated to the surgical field and business. Of Faith, he only had one concern.

"She won't stress me, nau?" he asked.

"She will cause no stress at all, and if she does then you hire someone else, because who in Nigeria doesn't need to line their pockets? She can stay in the boys' quarters and will do as you ask. To perfection."

"Okay then," the doctor replied. "No wahala."

"But you seem stressed. Why? Don't let this life stress you. You must learn how to laugh these things off, trust me, laughter keeps the devil away. Sullenness leads him right to your doorstep."

"It's not the devil I fear," he said.

With that, the doctor realized he had said more than he intended. Not because he didn't trust the old woman with his challenges, but because he realized that once he started addressing what stung him, he couldn't stop spewing his woes. Everyone was vexing him lately; one tenant had promised to raise two million naira to cover his cost of living for the next six months but had yet to acquire a contract that was supposed to "bring in the money." Another tenant was smoking in the room and the hallway reeked of marijuana, she had the nerve to ask for an extension hoping to pay by the end of the month instead of at a daily rate. The carpenter who had come to fix the cupboards did not fix all the cupboards and gave no good reason as to why, but still demanded a full day's payment for a quarter of the work. Kai! When one acquires an asset that sets you apart from the average Nigerian, everyone thinks you have become God and can clean up their messes.

He fended off the inclination to spill his hardships to Mrs. Bamidele, and tried to succinctly explain his overwhelm. "Shebi, what I'm finding in this venture of starting a guesthouse is that half of trying to run a business is making sure everyone understands that you are in fact running a *business*."

Faith could not forego the home service held every Monday. Nor would she leave immediately after their prayers when the tea and white bread with Blue Band margarine were served because a sinner could have a change of heart and ask for salvation. "Tell us, nau," she'd say, encouraging a member of the congregation to tell how Jesus had spoken something on their heart. "Talk nau. Speak nau."

She had given her testimony two Mondays ago to a captive audience. Nothing could have made her happier than to show her love of the Lord to those who stayed to listen.

See eh . . . my good friends, God is reliable. People may go but He will stay. See, if I didn't give my life to Him to hold, my enemies would have swallowed me by now. It was in the worship hall that I promised myself that nothing would swallow me whole o. I will be a loyal servant and serve in the church because I have received my appointment from the most high, sef.

She refused to negotiate whether to attend the Wednesday night service, that hallowed evening where people chose reverent murmuring over the usual shouting of the normal service. And of course,

Sunday she would have to excuse herself from morning till late afternoon. If the pastor was moved into an additional hour of worship, then who was she to stop him? Not to mention she'd be attending the nighttime vigil, the daytime vigil, the deliverance, the service trip to a village to pray with senior widows for comfort, and then the prayer pact program aptly named Seven Days of Intensity.

"Faith's not here." The doctor rubbed his mustache and sighed while he expressed his trouble. "She's gone more than she's here."

This unimpressive woman would sweep the floor one moment and the next there was no trace of her. She always came back later than intended, wearing that jacket with a handkerchief around her head.

He sat across from Arit, the young tenant from abroad who sat in befuddlement hearing the gossip. He knew that she had left a tiny studio where the lights went off for five days at a time. Eight generators whirred beneath her window and her small defunct gen was the loudest one. She wanted quiet in a building that was fairly new without any mold spreading across the ceiling. Mrs. Bamidele had taken a liking to her, which made the doctor shake his head, as she liked befriending women who came with a questionable history. The elder woman sat next to him wearing her usual look of concern when hearing that a business deal she had orchestrated no longer seemed promising. With a click of the tongue she said, *kilode!*

"I spoke to her about this church-at-every-hour rubbish," she said. "Bloody hell! Doesn't she know that faith without work is dead?"

"I even had to clean the kitchen this morning," the doctor added.

"Ta! You're joking."

"Madam, she's late all the time. This woman is really stressing my life, sha."

"Well then find someone else. Who in this country isn't looking to line their pockets?"

"They've paid vigilantes to go around the city hurling machetes at protesters. They'll kill anybody for the right amount. They're on the road she takes to meet her church, but she just can't be bothered. She's gone."

Mrs. Bamidele squirted honey into her cup of coffee before picking up steam again, "Do you know how many people in this country are looking to survive the hunger virus? No money coming in? Not even a kobo. Na wa."

"The thing is," the doctor said, "with all the energy she puts into her church, they should give her a small job, but they won't."

"Ha! Believe me you won't see me praying there ever again. In that welcome center where they have the sign that says Grace Hall, the c is missing. Can you believe that? With all the tithes the people give they won't find the money to buy a new letter. How can you say you are the shepherd that leads your flock if you cannot care about the small things? I tell you, if you cannot care about the small things that

can't talk, then how can you care about the numerous people in your church that can?"

The tenant sipped zobo, a drink that was deliv-
ered to her at the guesthouse every Wednesday since
her commandeering of the room with the balcony on
the top floor. She tapped her toes on the ground and
the doctor zeroed in on this action because it was a
similar tick he'd do during his Zoom classes when
the sweat on his neck drenched his collar and he was
too embarrassed to unbutton his shirt. The only
respite from the discomfort was to tap his feet since
no one could see him from the waist down. He observed her anxiety, but rather than making an event
of it, he was going to make a bigger splash tomorrow, when more guests would be tête-a-têting with
their eyes on the woman. He enjoyed playing tricks
and it was a joy to do this with a person who was too
new to spar. But maybe she could adapt? Come tomorrow—Friday—he'd find out. For now, he went
on bantering with the Madam.

"But that's exactly it!" he continued. "Women like
her, the common woman; they don't see it that way.
They'll give an entire salary to the church."

"Yes, well, God is everything to most people, almost to a fault I'd say . . ." Arit said, taking the last
gulp.

The doctor thought he would say no more on the
subject, but he couldn't help his need to state his
mind about the church-going woman. This unimpressive house help's absence unnerved him. It was
more than him needing her to sweep and iron. Yes,

it was partly that, as someone like him could pay someone like her to do small things for 500 naira a day. But the real question was, without her bustling and humming a gospel in the guesthouse, who would he be? And what would this country be without the millions of women who showed up to do the small things those who could pay, paid?

"A woman who worked as a house maid for a white family was very close to God," the doctor said. "She did good work, and the family took her to America. A few years later she came back to Nigeria a rich woman. You never know, sha. The small fish can become the big fish and no human has to understand why that's so. She has her reason for believing and that reason belongs to her."

Then came the silence.

"Well," the Madam said, eager to fill the void, "I pray—in Jesus Christ's name—that she doesn't become a dumb big fish. There are too many to count in this country."

A second later, Faith zipped through the door with no apologetic posturing for her lateness. Good afternoons were steadily exchanged and everyone's spirits lifted a tad.

"Your jacket," Mrs. Bamidele said, noticing that she was wearing a new outfit. "You're not wearing it, anymore?"

"No, ma," Faith replied. "The blazer's too tight. The buttons don't button, nau."

"You've been putting on some weight. All that swallow you chop when you think no one's looking.

195

Chewing the meat and only leaving the guests the bones. I tried eating from the ogbono today, it was a disgrace."

"Sorry, Mummy. The meat was going to spoil."

"And how would you know? And why not give us the meat instead of eat it yourself? My friend you better shut your mouth. Have you not just come from church and stood before God? And where's that jacket? Someone gives you a gift and you throw it away, just like that?"

"No, ma."

"You could have found a tailor to open the seam a bit to make it fit. You can't be picky. Who do you think you are, the Queen? You didn't throw it away, I hope?"

"No, ma."

"Greedy, girl."

"Sorry, ma."

"Bring it here."

"Ma?"

"I say go bring the jacket here, nau."

She hurried to get the item as Mrs. Bamidele said a few more words to berate her. But somehow, the insult hadn't hurt her an inch. A few hours ago she had stood before the Lord to tell Him she didn't have a care in the world and would not let this country kill her. The Madam included.

"Here, Ma," she said.

"What were you gonna do with it? Try to make some money off of it, huh? The salary the doctor gives you isn't enough?"

Another silence filled the room with Faith staring at the floor. It was clear to Mrs. Bamidele that the doctor and Arit would stay observers in the battle everyone knew the housemaid would lose. So she lashed at the quiet for the second time.

"Give the jacket to your Aunty. She'll take it," she ordered.

"That's okay," Arit spoke. "Really . . ."

"Why, nau?" the doctor asked in disbelief. "She can't wear the clothes of someone she doesn't know."

"Yes, she can," Mrs. Bamdiele said, keeping her glare on Faith. "A woman wearing the shirt of someone she doesn't know is the standard here. So long as it's not announced, who'd know the difference? You all think I'm being harsh but I must be harsh. Look at the stitching on that jacket. Look at the buttons. Look at the sleeves. This wasn't done by a regular jagga jagga tailor who can't be bothered, this was done by someone who cares. No one had to give anything to her. How else do you leave what's familiar and go somewhere new without a family or a friend? It's because somebody cares enough to give. If she can't appreciate what she's been given then she better stop wasting our time and give it to someone else. Bloody hell!"

Faith handed the blazer to the tenant. The tenant noticed the blazer wouldn't look half bad with the pair of faded jeans she had purchased the day before. She wasn't the Queen either, and would have to make do with what she had been given. The tenant had also realized she was older than the house-maid, and the realization that she had been her age once made the person cowering in front of her more flesh and blood. It was a recognition of this person not being more than a kid. She didn't want any of the house help's sanctimony to rub off on her if she decided to wear the coat. This was her only apprehension.

"I appreciate it, thank you," Arit said.

"Well done," said Mrs. Bamidele.

"But Madam," the doctor said, perplexed. "It's been worn, already."

"It'll be fine," Arit said quickly. "I've worn second hand clothes before."

"As I said, that's how most of the world gets along," the elder woman said. "We wear it because it fits, not because we want the story behind how it got to us. Believe me if you walk down the street right now in that blazer nothing will happen."

"Okay then," the doctor said. "It's fine."

"Yes, I believe it is."

Mrs. Bamidele took another sip of coffee, satisfied with herself.

The tenant patted the blazer while it lay on her lap.

"I'll go fix lunch, please," said Faith.

"Good timing," said the doctor.

"Well done. But you'll have to bring us snacks while we wait," said Mrs. Bamidele.

Faith went to the kitchen and began cutting a small onion in the palm of her hand. She delighted herself in thinking about how she would tell the doctor she had to leave in two days to attend a crusade to pray for widows in a nearby village. But she couldn't recall the name of the village she'd be going to.

Naïja

Nigeria, 2020. Arit.

If you were to ask my mother where she comes from, in true fashion, she'd start the story with her father. In truer fashion, she'd trace the story from what she knew of her father's father. She would tell of her father living in a village where *his* father had many, many wives.

"I am not talking about two or three." She'd tilt her head to the side and tap a hand on her knee, saying, "I am talking many-many."

She'd wiggle her nose to let you know there may be a slight judgment about *that* type of lifestyle.

"Can you count *many-many*?"

She isn't one to linger on sentiment for too long. On she'd go, telling you that her father's father was a very powerful man. A man who wrestled with the strongest of men and won each time. Men stronger and bigger than you and I could imagine. She'd say that *they* (and who knows who the mysterious *they* were) said her father's father made these large men squeal with the right headlock and pull of the arm. "You wouldn't want to fight him because you'd have to beat him."

No one wanted to fight him because they knew they couldn't beat him, which meant if they were going into the ring, they would either leave with the ultimate thrashing or be an inch away from dying. This is how she tells it, and it's the only time I see adoration sweep Mom's face. But I told you she's not one for lingering too long on a feeling.

"Peculiar," she'd say, drinking a cup of Earl Grey tea with almond milk (the healthier option for us who grew up on Lipton, evaporated milk, and oodles of white sugar). From what she was told, her father's father was a peculiar man. The rumors said that *her* father's father literally kept growing in size the more he fought and won against other men. Everyone was aghast, but no one said anything because he single-handedly fended off potential invaders of all shapes and sizes. Anyone wanting to take over the town would leave the place untouched because he was a lethal weapon. No one had strength enough to challenge such a man, and no one had the wherewithal to be this man's enemy. The villagers were content watching this man grow in strength, spirit, and size.

"Who could defeat a man like that?" Mom would ask.

"No one," we'd say.

"Who could defeat a man so strong?"

"Not us," we'd say.

"Then you may be surprised to know . . ."

Her voice would slightly rise as she said this. If you were there, you would see a smirk forming on her face as she told you that *her* father was the only one who could challenge a man as strong as *his* father. How, you might wonder?

"He changed," she'd say.

Her father was not as tall as *his* father, nor was he as strong as his father, and *her* father's mother was not one of his father's favorite wives, making it nearly impossible for him to ever be the favorite son. Still, he became a force to reckon with when he walked sixteen miles to the closest missionary school, took on a Christian name, Daniel, and returned to the village denouncing everything his father said or did as primitive. That'll make a big giant fall hard, when you come to the said giant's doorstep and call out their entire life as totally irrelevant.

And this was the day—my mother says—life really began. It was when my mother's father chose to step away from the magic. Her father took more steps towards the city, where he was able to serve as a superintendent of schools. He married one wife and had children who went to proper schools and grew to find respectable work in actual buildings. Sundays were for church with a cross on front and a picture of Jesus inside (and you can guess what their Jesus looked like).

"I've got no silver or gold to give you," she'd say. "But we come from a people that walked sixteen miles away from the past to find a future. Isn't that an honorable quest? It's that same spirit that brought us here."

Our chat is more fruitful these days, her words, rather than creating distance, intrigue. I've always regarded this story as one of the most irksome she's ever told. To only trace existence down from one man to another, with the complete erasure of the women who bore them, well, this is a story lacking all sense. But on this soil I have access to the girl she was. Her wails, her disappointments, those small pleasures that put her at ease, those things are closer, no longer an elusive machination that can't be caught. It can be swallowed, happily digested in the belly until one is satiated with delight, and thus my ears are open when she tells this particular story because it feels familiar.

She must have been a meek girl, with her particular nature, because not everyone is born knowing how to put pressure on the world around them, so I have concluded that someone put pressure on her. Most women learn, some women don't, and my mother is the woman who didn't know how. Not until she had an ocean between her and the world in question. She has become more real to me, the further away I get. This place is for the bold, preferably for those who are happy dominating the weak, so how do shy girls dreaming of other universes fare in the fatherland*?

"How far in the past are you gonna go?" she asks.

"As far as I can," I say.

"And what if you find it's all rotten?"

*Nigerians often refer to their country as the fatherland

And the only answer to give is the one that will bruise her the most, because I've come to find that my inability to toe the line wounds. Our fated clash comes down to this: She looks forward to some far off peak or horizon turned away from it all, and I, her daughter, have turned back to see what was left.

"Then I'll go beyond that," I answer.

"You'll see how we've failed you," she says after a minute. "Where you are is a big question mark."

But I've dealt with her since, quite sternly and without regard for the sacrifices she made giving a new country every drop of herself so her children could speak that good English grammar. And no one will hear these conversations because I've been trained not to speak against my mother. But the day I learned she could be touched and grabbed, I gripped her and squeezed tight until her sincerity came out.

"You were weak once," I told her. "You know what it's like to be afraid."

She still says I never told her anything about what occurred. But I know better. She spent much time under the covers in my girlhood, and we both know why she hid there. And she shouldn't be angry now, she's got no authority to have a shred of rage in my direction. All she's ever done is packed a suitcase and left people behind. She gets it. She lives tucked far in the woods in a small New England town for God's sake.

I was hesitating to kill a roach when we last spoke. It sprinted across the room, trying to find a dank crevice to slip into, that's when she rang. It was a hopeless conversation between us as her mood completely mismatched my own.

"Why are you still there?" she asked. "You weren't that far from achieving something worthwhile before you disappeared." I moved from the mattress to the couch, hoping my elevation would save me from the critters.

"You and I both know that's a lie," I answered. It was an unconscionable lie, as she knew what had happened a few months before I left.

She's gotten a new nose piercing. A tiny circle in the left nostril put in by a burly tattooed man named Tully. She says the sting of pain caused by that small ring anchors her to the Bay.

Then she got a tattoo, a bunch of pink roses with purple stems on her foot. Right on that part of the foot where you have that big bone. That's where the debauchery starts, and it goes all the way to her big toe. Never have I poked a hole through my nostril or gotten a drawing carved on top of a bone to prove that I'm brave. But it wouldn't make sense to judge her anymore than I already do. The truth is that we secretly detest each other, possibly because the other wants to jump inside the other's skin, prove the other can live the other person's life more adeptly if only there was an opportunity.

She walks around the city with her emotional support puppy, Pepper, sporting a fresh buzz cut, happily fitting into the landscape as she gallivants with all the markers of a Bay area broad. The murals in the Mission, the parks with people sitting on the ground, the taquerias with samba music booming while you're crossing the street, that's her.

"Pick up from where you left off," she said, doubling down. "Nigeria can jade you. Our parents have been telling us for decades. Sure we have nostalgia but life's about having sense. Why suffer? You're a single woman who has lived in the Bay for eight years."

"I've heard this before."

"So then what are you doing? You were supposed to visit Kenya for six weeks not turn this into a quest. You got no people where you are other than that overbearing lady you hang around—"

"Mrs. Bamidele."

"And how long is that gonna last?"

"We can talk about something else."

"But what's with you?" she asked. "Can you really move forward in that part of the world being the way you are?"

She's become cooler towards me, reminding me of the San Francisco breeze that nips at you even if you wear a sweater.

"That jacket you were wearing in the picture you texted," she began, "I saw one exactly like it when I went thrifting with Lonnie and Derron. They say hello by the way . . ."

I had asked her if I looked good in the new gift bestowed upon me, but instead she used the moment to express her disappointment. She's become a woman of the do. Do a grant, do a film project, do a political protest, do anything but go back to where the person closest to you lost her clothes only to leave you.

Another roach scurried across my big toe. The first had been allowed to go unscathed out of a misplaced benevolence. Spraying the room with repellent could have provided a solution, but then I'd sniff the poison too. I grew irritated that my life was now bound up with the roach. Through the window I saw that the house across the street was well lit and heard its generator going. Everyone has a generator to light the place when NEPA* goes. My rinky-dink contraption often loses steam because it's shoddy. The guys who sold it to me at that warehouse swore on their mothers it was in perfect condition.

If I were to tell her what I could—if she would listen—I'd tell her it began with a cockroach. My will to stay began with the tiny insect whose life I hesitate to splatter with a flip flop. I'd tell her about my first week in the tiny apartment, how the fan blew hot air as I danced in front of the mirror wearing my silk robe to some funk song playing on the phone. When the song ended my tummy had grumbled and I went to the kitchen. On the counter, crawling about my beef suya, was a roach. I was sickened to see something else trying to get to it, as eating the beef was like chewing on well seasoned contentment. It had been stored in a container as I did not

*Power holding company of Nigeria

yet have a working fridge, but since I had only spotted one roach, I quickly decided that it was merely a small intrusion.

The more irksome challenge that evening was that the lantern would soon go off because the battery had run out, which meant that in a few hours I'd be in complete darkness. The electricity had just shut off and my gen was too defunct to be useful. The second critter came, a bigger, more grotesque specimen than the first. I had shut the kitchen door hoping that if more roaches were lurking they wouldn't cross the boundary I set. I quickly sat cross-legged on the couch. Then came the third. From the bathroom. Then came the fourth hurrying out with the fifth. And then the sixth, already racing about with the seventh, both daring to glide across the wall. The gall they had. And I was terrified, because one day I'd have to annihilate them all and not feel bad about it. It had been like this for a month, killing a few and letting the majority go to keep the death toll low. But she never cares to ask about life here, and this is the fundamental difference between us. For her, the present is in a thrift store on Market Street, and for me, it's the place where my parents left.

Three months later I feel more trapped speaking to her than I do with the insects. The roach would have been spared that night, if it hadn't rested on the teal robe with the red flowers, the one I had danced in my first night at the apartment. It was the only memento saved from Nkechi's world. She had given me that robe after she decided to wear that long striped T-shirt for a nightgown.

The phone fell as I lunged towards the roach that had flown to the wall. She yelled through the phone, asking if anyone was there, sounding muffled and panicked somehow. I sensed an undertone of seething in the way she said hello. It was similar to the latent indignation I had been nursing for months, a sort of rage that kept me focused on killing a flying roach. I smashed the roach's guts against the wall until it split into three parts: The legs, the body, and the head. I hung up the phone, deciding to text her the next day to say there was a bad connection.

The Second Husband

The United States, 2020. Uduak.

He had a booming voice that caused her heart to pump quickly, and when he first saw her and blurted, "I love you," she jumped. It had been after a year with no one to hold, a daughter gone, and when he said *that*, she heard her heart beat. He wore glasses, carried a book in his briefcase, and kept a small Webster's dictionary on his work desk. By the looks of it he appeared focused, and this was a better prospect than the louse who had been thrust on her in her first marriage. This man's dictionary was his companion in a land of so many unfamiliar words and she yearned for definition in the country she had committed herself to. He was intelligent and prideful, which meant he had the capacity to out-think the naysayers saying he'd never make any-thing of himself because of the way his mind worked. His people had a word to describe his odd disposition: Mad. And the mad ones never made it

out. They were pariahs. Demented, insane, inca-
pable of keeping one's self in tact. They never expected him to make it so far. His side of the family
chose not to tell her about how her soon-to-be-hus-
band walked listlessly in the darkness and came
back in the morning with his eyes bloodshot saying
he was hungry.

They were in a new land and surely could forget
all that had come before; there were new perils to
face, and it was becoming colder where they were
and he had said he'd be there for her, and she was
still young enough to start a family that could make
the people back home say she wasn't damaged.

He rambled to himself on the toilet, rambled
while trimming his beard, rambled while washing
the plates, and though she found it odd, she thought
he'd one day cool off. She couldn't have known he
would become a terror, to her, to the innocent ones
yet to be born, this is what she tried to tell her second daughter from her second marriage, the one
who had left her, unlike Ekom and Okon who visited
often to cook meals, watch TV, and rake the leaves.
Her second was impatient, unable to listen to how
her father, for all his flaws, was a man hunting for
answers, and that her mother was hunting too.

She wasn't interested in how her mother had
spent nights kneeling down over the bed, weak from
the pummeling she had taken in the last year as she
prayed and said, I'm exhausted. The others cared,
Ekom, Okon, but the second daughter was belliger-
ent in her questioning, asking, "Did you know what

happened?" And when Uduak tried to explain who her father was when she met him the daughter cut her off. "I won't hear another word," she said. "If you start the story with him it'll drive a wedge between us, he may be your center but he's not mine." Uduak, not quite knowing where else to begin, became resigned, and said, "Best I be quiet then."

The Intercession

Nigeria, 2020. Arit.

"Still in bed?" Mrs. Bamidele barged in, carrying a smoking incense burner. The fruity scent could choke you if you were in the smog for too long. I had been plucking away at the computer till very late, but she didn't take this as legitimate work. She referred to my type of work as brain work, shrugging it off as involving "too much grammar." She had read one of my articles once, mildly irritated. "You Westerners give headaches. If you're talking about the weather then you must describe every detail of what you think: The weather was blistering hot and because of that I sweat through my shirt and then became dehydrated, and because I was dehydrated I couldn't very well walk to the park so I took a cab and that is why I am here now, standing before you. That's how you all do it. But us, we'll say: The heat no go kill me. Why show off and make this exercise?" To her, work meant wearing slacks and going into an air-conditioned office for eight hours. Or staying in the kitchen washing ugu leaves and grinding pepper for a soup. My job was to edit articles and produce a product that sounded like the reporter had been trained in the UK. It was a search for clarity, preening whatever shrouded the sentence, a daunting process that required a literary overhaul when sifting through the errors:

HAWKING COLLAPSE INTO WORSENING CRISIS

> The fact of modernity is that Nigeria is a country where the rich continue to amass the spoils for themselves. But for regular Nigerian it is wholly impossible to feed and find work. This according to a representative speaking on behalf of Hawkers who risk an onslaught of Police Harassment and Extortion of the highest levels.

I had since moved out from the studio, rented for me by the publication that had given me the best their naira could afford. My food had spoiled my last day there. The okra soup, once a fresh green color, had a pasty film covering it, with a corner turning a chalky white. When stepping outside, the smell of trash broiling in the sun nearly overtook me, and I wondered what had been tossed into the dumpster that morning. Passerbys threw everything in there, a black trash bag full of moist leaves and split wood, bath slippers, tufts of hair, sanitary pads, wasted food, these items roasting in the heat. And when the sun went down it would be a night of watching for the crawlers, the numbers were fewer, but I was appalled at the way I enjoyed smashing them. It was getting harder to say I was acting in self-defense.

I had moved into a three-story house with an industrial-sized fridge, a generator, and an inverter for the compound, whose other residents included a young man who opened and closed the gate, Faith—the housekeeper who was usually at church—and another woman who lived in a smaller house and peeked out the curtains every so often. Her name was Patricia. A woman with slits for eyes and a thin mouth who had the countenance of someone who could not be bothered. The owner of the guesthouse insisted on sleeping in the boys quarters so he would never lose money on a room. He occasionally used the parlor to host meetings with a group of heavily cologned men who were looking to go in on some construction deal. When the gathering ended, he'd groan about the money he wasted to show his appreciation for the guests who would possibly let him in on a contract.

It was here that I met her, sitting at the dining table with trays of food laid out. It was a chance encounter since a minute before I had pondered whether to find Joe—the man opening and closing the gate—to tell me where to buy some fruit. I hadn't said much, but she said, "Sit down. Eat," and so I did.

She barges in when I'm on the phone, on the toilet, and sleeping. I could likely do the same to her, as she prefers such closeness, but I've never done so. When she was teaching me how to turn eba, an uneasiness about her began. I reached for the spoon to turn it, but she insisted on turning the garri with her hand, kneading the water and grain into a gelatinous ball. The spoon would have gotten the same result, but my urge to tell her this lessened when I noticed she was gleeful.

"It's okay." She smiled after I declined to eat from the same bowl of soup as her, opting to warm up my own. "You're like my first daughter, reserved. I raised her to stick up her nose and speak good English. I paid a high price to make her who she was and I got my money's worth. She was a good girl. Rest her soul."

Her latest gripe is that I'm losing too much weight. "You're not eating well which is why you toss around when you sleep. You must eat well for the night or else you'll dream of spirits chasing you. This happened to my younger brother Bayo but then he began taking swallow at night and slept well. You could drop him anywhere and when it was time to sleep, so long as he'd eaten well, he was fine."

She puts the burner on the rug as the smoke fills the room.

"Do you want tea?" she asks.

"No."

Out the door she walks, and then comes back with Lipton tea and a bowl of peanuts placed in the middle of the sunflower-shaped platter with the crack tearing through one of the petals. She places the tray at the foot of the bed.

"You know, Giorgia's dead," she says, before walking out.

"What?" I ask.

She walks out the door, humming. I remove the covers and follow her to the kitchen.

"They say she had malaria."

"Are they sure it wasn't covid?"

"Of all things to die from in this country. Malaria? A woman like her? Is a lie."

"Was the husband there when she died?"

"They say he was around while she was getting treatment."

"You know she was trying to leave him."

"An African man can never let his wife leave, dear. It's not possible. He'd rather find a way for both of you to die together than let you go."

She places a small plate of puff puff on the ironing board.

"Eat," she says, frowning slightly. "You forgot to bring your tea and peanuts. I'll be back."

Thirty seconds later she's back.

"She said he'd kill her."

"Well . . ." She sighed. "It's her rich friends to blame, really. If they could have helped they should have. Now they'll come out saying they were her friends but we all know they couldn't be bothered."

"She asked me for help," I said.

Mrs. Bamidele nearly choked.

"My dear," she scoffs. "What help can you give, when you are here managing your life? Are you rich?"

"No," I reply.

"Then for these purposes you two weren't friends. Friendship must come with financial benefits in her case."

I cracked a warm peanut between my teeth, spat out the shell, and chewed the flesh.

"How does a white woman end up like this?" I ask.

"Oh, but she wasn't white anymore, dear. She gave that up." Mrs. Bamidele leaned against the counter. "She married a Yoruba man, took his Yoruba name, had his Yoruba children, children who look more like the husband than her by the way, and for decades did what a Nigerian woman must do to acquire the standard she wants. The past was far behind her."

I rest my chin on a fist.

"Nothing in life goes simply does it?"

"And why would it," she said, inhaling another puff puff. "If it were simple then it wouldn't be life."

Giorgia had owned a cafe, one of the nicest in town. Inside were blood-orange chairs made of velvet, with serpentine designs swirling on the wooden handles. Shag rugs for the sitting areas and Latin jazz played in the background. The chef would bake a batch of biscottis every morning for customers to nibble with a hot drink. The place smelled like cinnamon and orange peel for a good while until it trailed into something else. Her favorite coffee to recommend was that one from Haiti. It was bitter, smelled like dirt, and got you wired with one sip. She knew most of the farms growing coffee in the country and for her it was a point of excitement, but her enthusiasm didn't seem to matter to most people because most people preferred tea. And if they wanted coffee they would request a sachet of Nescafé. I had watched four people demand Nescafé in place of the forty-two coffee blends displayed on the shelf. They became further aggravated when the waiters refused to take their money to fetch a bundle of coffee sachets from the small kiosk down the road. She had said if she didn't have her children to worry about she would sleep in the office in the back, which was a sad remark to hear because a woman over six feet tall would never make it in a room like that. I told her to get a pillow and sleep on the big couch between the velvet chairs, but she objected, fearing someone would pass by and see a woman sleeping outside her home. And there would be no greater shame than that.

It was my hope that Giorgia would have followed Aggie's suit. Marura had sent me a message alerting me that she was back at the hostel with no husband in sight. "Thought you'd be interested to hear . . ." she texted. Rather than drinking herself into oblivion she got herself a single room and spent two weeks snorkeling and ordered grilled fish by the pool. If Giorgia had done this, ridded herself of all expectation, she would have had to undergo an unpleasant reconstruction. Give up the last name she used to survive in a new country and relinquish the status that comes with marriage. Such an undertaking robs one of their glamour. Possibly she could have taken the risk, she would have lost it all but she'd still be alive. It was this meandering thought that caused me to cry.

"Why the tears?" Mrs. Bamidele whispered. She had a way of turning up when you thought no one was around. I was sure I had locked the door.

She opened the blinds as though it was daylight.

"Didn't your parents teach you not to cry alone?" she nearly yelled. "Why cry? You're feeding, we're living comfortably, no covid has reached this place. People are dropping around us but we're alive. Why has crying become your portion?"

She sits on the bed.

"Maybe you didn't eat well. Should I warm some moi moi for you?"

I shake my head no.

"What is it, then?" She stares at me with her eyes which happen to be a dull sky blue, although I do not know how they got that way. I pull the comforter over my chest before sitting up.

"I already have a spirit chasing me," I say.

"Eh-heh." She grunts. "Good or evil?"

"No clue."

"Man or woman?"

"Woman."

"Young or old?"

"Older than me, younger than many."

She cradled my face between her hands, drawing her forehead closer to mine and said, "You are far too blank about this spirit. It's a problem." She gave me a slight push then added, "Spirits are sent to jolt you, and it won't stop till you wrestle with it. You've got to hold it down and talk to it, you understand? Chase it through the wee hours of the night if you have to. Whatever you need to do to relieve yourself, you do that, but whatever you do, don't let it haunt you. It'll haunt you forever and disrupt your peace. If it comes charging, you better charge too. Run faster, show her you aren't afraid of death. In fact, when you first saw her, you should have beat her well-well, punched her down, and said, 'I will deal with you.'"

"I was eight," I said.

"And then? Another eight-year-old would have dealt with her since," she said. After waiting a few seconds she resumed her prattling, "Are you sure you don't want moi moi? Extra pepper was put in it. It'll spark you up."

"No thank you, ma," I replied. "I am full."

"Okay o."

Her refusal to let go caused discomfort, which she must have recognized because her grip tightened as she squished my face inward, perhaps trying to shift a resistant quality that was etched in my nature. The woman was notorious for doing the thing that annoyed one the most. In our months together,

her gift of nagging defied all bounds, so much that people acquiesced to her will or ran away. I would have argued with her to give me some air, but her voice is emboldened by any provocation. Mine would have been too thin to combat her, and I wasn't raised to argue at 3 a.m.

"What has been the primary thrust of your conversations with her?" she asked.

"We danced a bunch and she'd often ask about my mother."

"Ay-ya!" she said, standing up to pace the room. "You better ask your Mom. Tell her exactly what this spirit looks like. She won't tell you everything because no mother can. But it'll relieve some constraint from her, because that same constraint harasses you. You understand?"

"The same thing that killed Giorgia killed the spirit," I said.

"And what was that?" She raised her eyebrow and stood still.

"Stress."

"Oh, but dear you must get over it. Stress is the standard."

She put her hand on my head, as if she was checking for a fever.

"I'll get the broom to sweep the house." She patted my arm.

"It's clean," I said.

"Not with the regular broom. The special broom. That one you saw in my closet. It'll sweep all those funny-funny spirits away, similar to how we sweep away funny-funny insects. It's quite possible to address these types of problems. Is this not Nigeria?"

It was a thatched broom the women wearing handkerchiefs and orange overcoats used to sweep the roads in the morning. They had to crouch low to pack up the dust and grit, charged with doing this for the whole estate. Quite a number of houses have this broom tucked in the corner. Which could mean everyone has a spirit they're trying to sweep away.

"Kpele," Mrs. Bamidele said. "I'm surprised your parents never told you, but that's how it goes when we raise our kids abroad thinking it's the answer. But relax, okay? This country will not swallow you whole, your portion will not be Giorgia's."

The Guide

A parallel universe. Ekpewan.

My Guide sounds old but when you get to meet her, you'll see she is very much alive. Think of all the old people's voices you've heard put together in one. That's her. Old people have harder voices, they're not as sweet as a young person who hasn't lived so long and who may not sound like anyone yet. Her voice can be gentle and well-meaning, but mainly rough, and it grinds on you when she wants to pester you. When you meet her you'll also see that she talks too much. She can't close her mouth because no one listened to her when she was human. People ignored her and pretended they didn't need her. That's how she explains the whole thing. It was a life where as soon as she got old and her children got a taste of a new culture they began ignoring their elders. She says all the mistreatment led her to lose her sight. But no one can be perfectly right all the time. So I think that maybe she ended up not seeing because she wanted things to stay the same and they didn't. Just my opinion.

When you meet her, you'll also see she doesn't have much meat on her arms but this doesn't mean she's weak. Those arms have pounded afang leaves for a nice soup. Soup she enjoyed making for one of her daughters, because it was her daughter's favorite soup, and then that soup became the soup her daughter made for her daughter, and so the women in our family enjoy afang soup, but generally we like any soup with plenty of green leaves. I don't know how my Guide is related to me yet, but I'm sure we're related somehow. I should have recognized her but since I had so much pain from the life I lived I don't remember her. I truly believed that when I met Jesus, a pack of angels would greet me by beating my bum bum with a stick and then drag me into the water to wash me clean. But then I heard the sobs from the baby I had ruined and I couldn't find her to soothe her like a Mummy would. This was punishment o.

My Guide says that soon the forgetfulness will go away and I'll know what to call her. She says when I can see who she is she'll know some of my pain has gone. So for now, I call her my Guide. She hovers over me like a hawk and has not left my sight since I've arrived. She says she won't abandon me, but we'll see, people are weird and the spirit world is weirder. But going it alone without those that care for you and without God as we've recognized Him to be is frightening.

She likes to show me different people, people who must be my family though I can't tell you their names. One time she took me to a baby girl who was sitting on a blanket on the floor while a woman was pounding leaves with a wooden stick to prepare a soup. When she finished, she put the leaves on her finger for the girl to taste and the girl twisted her mouth before spitting the leaves out all over her chin. Then the woman fed her a spoon of palm oil and then some stock fish. But do you know how she fed the girl the fish? She chewed the fish in her mouth and then spat the paste onto her palm to feed the baby. My Guide asked me if I knew who she was and I said no. She sucked her teeth and said, "We have to fix this problem. Or else how will your child know you?"

It was our mother. I only knew Mum from that photo I kept under my pillow. I didn't know she existed outside of that picture. I didn't know she was once helpless.

My Guide often brings me to a garden she used to take care of. The plants are withered and dry now because the money to maintain the place is finished, but there are still some orange flowers that arch towards the back door, and they are very alive and pretty. I believe plants should stretch towards the sun, but to these flowers, the woman who guides me must have been the sun. They perked up for her whenever she'd come from the back door. They continue to perk up for her because she still visits the garden frequently.

My Guide says I interfered with you too much. Sorry about that.

I still follow you around, can't help it, you are fun to watch and since you wouldn't talk to me, your dreams were where I could get a hold of you. I fixed a good plan for you to hear a glimpse of what happened to me, to show you we were the same. I turned off the switch on the memory so you wouldn't see and left you in darkness. All you heard were his grunts and you mistook my pain for yours. I guess I see why, violation tends to make the same sound.

When you ran down the street with all of yourself flapping in the wind, I began working on your behalf. I'm telling you these things as I am now, not as I was when you drove me away. Since then I've been told I interfered with you too much. Sorry, eh?

I lie with your mother when she's under the bedding. She didn't take my death well, and though I'm no longer human, she's happy I'm there. I won't tell you what I say to her and what she says to me. But we feel the same way about you.

Just so you know, an ancestor can't be thrown away. You may dislike us, it's allowed, but you can never really send us away, this is not allowed. Since we're all eating from the same stew if the meat in the stew is rotten then we all taste the same flavor. You get?

Arit

Nigeria, the present.

Some call me akata to convey, she's one of us, but not really one of us, but yet not really one of them. Phil—Mrs. Bamidele's driver—calls me oyingbo. A touch kinder, I suppose. Says he can tell from my hands that this place isn't my country. That's what he said to me as I struggled to get into the car because the handle was stuck. "Oyingbo grip," he laughed. "Weak. The American standard." When the dust coats my shoes and I greet people with "Good morning, ma," or "Good afternoon, sir," people take me more as one of them. I've rid myself of the bum shorts and spaghetti straps I used to roam around in. The mandate of *thou shall cover thyself* subconsciously pervades. I've seen women in 100-degree weather covered from head to toe with the sun at its zenith, walking like they were gliding on air.

A tailor sewed a few dresses for me and I explained to her that the dress needed to come in at the waist and the bust line needed to dip past the collar bone. She chided me about calling too much attention to myself. "This dress will make a good impression," she said. "You're new here, you'll see."

I told him, Suleiman, about this small disappointment I endured. "Looks like you found yourself a church tailor," he said.

One of his knuckles has slid down his hand, reminding me of rolling a bowling ball down a lane. I enjoy rubbing my finger inside the dip, stopping when I meet the bump. There is no acceptable title for what we are yet. Labels like boyfriend, girlfriend, and partner don't hold weight in the same way that Mr., Mrs., wife, and husband do. For now, we've settled on friends. I wished he was in the car to coach me on how to speak to Mrs. Bamidele's driver who speaks to me like I'm completely inept.

"Pick up your phone," the driver demands. His tone is rough to the ears which makes hearing him a great effort.

"It's normal for people to call twice if you don't pick the first time," he says, making me ponder if his brashness is a way of showing concern.

"I've noticed," I reply.

"Ignoring people isn't always a good way. With people comes opportunity. If they aren't asking for money then you should pick their call." His eyes darted from me to the road. "Are they asking for money? If they're asking you to dash them you must reject their call. It is your right. Okay?"

I draft letters in a notepad, writing the revelations that come with leaving a life for a new one.

Nkechi,

Phil warns me about tempting the devil.
If a house help is near, hide your valuables.
When driving, lock the doors.
If you're rich, walk poor.
But everyone tempts the devil.
Plus, I got dirt on Phil.
I've been sent to watch him.

The phone rang again. He shifted his attention to another driver that did not signal he'd be crossing the lane.

"This man is not acting normal. At all. Kai!" We passed street sweepers and a man selling oranges at the bottom of the hill.

"You talk like them but you look like us so naturally you'll see more of the reality than they can," he said, noticing how I was staring at the blonde woman in a baseball cap and shorts jogging across the street. "You must realize who you are, or else it'll be tough. It's just like that." He rolled down his window to chastise someone driving on the opposite side of a one-way lane. *See now, you are driving through oncoming traffic. You are driving like a woman. Stupid man.* A few minutes later we were waiting in front of a red light with fifty seconds on the timer. Phil surveyed the road, driving underneath the stoplight blinking red. He was impatient but attempting to exercise restraint. I too am eager to deliver these Ghana-Must-Go bags filled with Mrs. Bamidele's high heels from Lagos and we still must buy her provisions. I'm in no dire hurry, but I'd like to use the bathroom. The driver may have sensed my urgency because he tapped the steering wheel and said while pushing the brake, *"I just dey waste my time here, abeg I wan commot."*

Phil says that if there's any emotional message one must send, then they should do so on Whatsapp, because you can state your diatribe without interruption. I had been waiting for Suleiman to admit it. You love me? Say it. This is what I had texted. This man that I had chosen to love had a wife and two children stuffed in a gated house in a town I had never visited. If he was to make me a cliché—a woman in love with a man who belonged to someone else—he had better say this. They tell a woman who meets a single man to watch out for a wife and a few kids to pop out because he'll have no choice but to claim them when the ruse is up. But at the very least, the man with a knuckle that slid down his index finger, must admit that a bond was there, even if the memory of this relationship will eventually be scrubbed away. He soon called.

"Should I come over? So we'll talk?"

"No."

"Why not?"

"Because we won't talk."

"Then, now what?"

"We end it."

"Obviously, it was always headed there," he sighed. "But how should we do this?"

I paused.

"I love you," he said.

Feeling a bit more satisfied, I answered, "Not sure it matters."

When we last kissed, it was as if he was trying to consume me. A neediness with every tongue stroke enveloped me. His skin was usually warm and perspiring, with his lips slightly chapped. But when we kissed his lips were a bit cooler, and that's how I realized something between us had shifted. The next day the rain came.

I think of her—my friend—and scribble:

Nkechi,

The man with the sliding knuckle says it's rude to talk feelings when the majority can't feed.

But then where do the feelings go?

I conclude that the people are eating their feelings.

P.S.
He wore a wig and lipstick.
It was Halloween.
Just for fun.

He swore no one else would see him like that.

He doesn't want to feel shunned.

I kissed him.

Told him, no judgement.

I've let her know a little bit about him. Not that he's married but just that I'm in trouble. When she texted, Did you find someone you love?, I replied: Think so.

She sent a voice note of herself cackling. That was the entire message, a minute of her in raucous laughter tearing down the years she endured of my self-righteousness and judgement.

He's a devout Muslim and is bound to his sense of duty. I have no real understanding of what it means to come from somewhere and feel bound to that place. I suppose I lost this chip in the hustle and bustle of American living, trying to sort out how to integrate into the chaotic fabric I was raised in. I was ensconced in the things that can perplex someone who is constantly hyphenated, am I this or that? I have given up so much to become myself that at times it's easier to identify as nothing.

He clings to these identifiers, carrying the grief that holding so tight can bring. If ideas of family and duty have to go I'll move on and carry the grief of the absence. No matter how you slice it, wherever there's a choice there's a loss. Our beliefs clash as we joust for whose way is right.

"You don't mention him," he says.

"Who?"

"Your father. You've mentioned visiting the rest of them if you decide to go back but what of your father? We don't do that here. Subtract the father."

"I've told you."

"He's half of you, yeah? You can't throw away half of you."

"I've taken the bits I like."

"So you'll blot the rest of him out?"

I lay his head on my chest, squeezing him into my body as I crouch to meet his ear. "If I spend one more minute thinking how a hopeless man committed a hopeless act because of a hopeless situation, then I fear this hopeless story won't get anymore interesting."

"So you'll forget?" he asked, incredulously.

"No. I just won't dwell on him. You get?"

Phil slows the slightly rundown 2012 Peugeot near a group of people selling groundnuts, avocados, bananas, and pawpaw. I give an extra 1500 to buy biscuits for myself and Faith. She's with Mrs. Bamidele, turning amala and microwaving okra soup, no doubt. Phil's the designated money handler because it's easier for him to haggle a good price. When I speak, the price goes up. But Mrs. Bamidele was adamant on sending the money to me, to send to Phil. "It's so he knows what the hierarchy is," she said. "Are you not my daughter?" She calls me her daughter, but I'm not her biological daughter, but everyone mistakes me for her daughter because we have bulging eyes, long necks, and flat feet.

Perhaps with her children gone, she aims to pour herself into the gaps she saw in the way I barely mentioned my father and spoke of my mother with a yardstick of distance. She saw pictures of my siblings on my phone, but she caught they were not recent photos because she stated, "You look younger, more fat on your cheeks . . ." She wants me to get married and even called a pastor to fly from Lagos to help me with my "issue." She grabs me whenever she can to tell me that I will not become a spinster. "Now, Arit," she says, "Chinaza asked for a husband and says the spirit told her to set a date. She is forty-three and well preserved so it's obvious that God has kept her because life hasn't mishandled her. She's setting the date for August ninth of next year and we know—in Jesus name—that her husband will come. Now Arit, do you have the same ability to tap into this power with the Holy Spirit? Or should I call the pastor to go into the spiritual realm and look into this for you?"

I'd politely decline, but the pastor has already phoned to pray with me about my spinsterhood.

I write a note:

Nkechi,

I met Mrs. Bamidele's second daughter. Funmilayo.

She's leaving for Brooklyn because her mother won't stop pulling her strings.

She says I should be careful.

Since I'm the new daughter.

With expectations there are no free lunches in Freetown.

Her mother wants her married. Three children. Minimum.

Funmilayo looked at me once and said, see me.

I saw her.

She's not getting married.

P.S.

Did you know she sent her to a village school?

When the middle school teacher told her Funmilayo insisted on being called Fran.

She bought a one way ticket from JFK to Naija.

Told her daughter go be Fran in the village.

Phil handed me a bushel of bananas, a bottle of groundnuts, and carried the avocados and pawpaw. "The money don finish," he said.

"Did Mummy send you more money?" I shook my head no. He got in the driver's seat and I the passenger's.

When seated in the car I jot in the notepad.

Nkechi,

Getting money is the Nigerian's love language.

Mrs. Bamidele is convinced that Phil is stealing. She'll give him 4,000 to buy from the market, and he'll skim 1,000 off the top, that type of hustle. It's a country of the rich, the poor, and the dwindling middle class. People do what they must when options are few, and a mind constantly chasing money is the order of the day.

Everyone hangs around her, whispering, "This one has money o." But when we talk, she says she's underfunded, which is baffling, given that she sent Phil 30,000 to get a carload of items solely for her comfort. "They are mistaken," she says. "My budget is low, nau! See, I gave my brother one million naira and he promised he'd give it back in full next week, and since then he has not called to say he's made the transfer to my account. I texted him to say he has offended me and then he sends me a picture of a disgusting rip in his foot saying he's been in the hospital for surgery and I say, 'Ah-ah!—what is this? Why frighten me with this horror show when I'm asking for my money, nau?' But I'm not worried about him, sha. You don't smash a fly with a sledgehammer."

She's a retired commander. The police salute her at the checkpoints when they see the army sticker on the car. "I went from selling agidi in Surelere to climbing the ranks," she said. "To come home without enough money meant a beating, so I stayed out there until I met a man who handed me 1,000 naira and said God would bless me to make something of myself one day. Haven't I done that?" She was supposed to be given a title higher than commander, but she was never given that.

I've put the phone on vibrate. It buzzes when we're examining the pawpaw (two smalls for 800 naira) and Phil looks annoyed that I am screening the call. He knows that I've screened his calls before, but that's alright, we all screen first and answer later when necessary. Suleiman and I have agreed the way we ended it is for the best. If I hear his voice one more time I'll think of her. His wife. The woman who signed up for that title. And then her kids. They who didn't sign up for anything.

Phil and I lugged all the items into the kitchen of the new apartment, and we laid out a tiny store on the counter. When inspecting the bananas, Mrs. Bamidele sucked her teeth. "These bananas are no good," she said, peeling off the skin to taste. "They boiled them to force their ripeness. They're soft but not sweet. Goodness, anything for a kobo. Nigeria, we are such wonderful people, eh?"

She always spotted the miss of excellence. Those greens I sautéd her, with efo and tomatoes, she could taste the few specks of sand. An inattentive palate would miss it but not her. I usually rinsed the veggies for about eight minutes, but in my laziness I hadn't rinsed them for that long. When she let me know about the specks she tasted I was embarrassed because that meant she had tasted my laziness.

After each item was reviewed, she handed Phil 1,500 naira to compensate him for two hours.

When they had first met she had paid him 25,000 for the day, but then as soon as she called him her son, and he called her Mum, the payments got slimmer. He'd take 10,000 for the day, driving on a near-empty tank. By the end of his shift, after he got to Lugbe and checked his account, he was fuming. I know this because he tells me so. Riding with him is like going to a confessional, he'll look in the mirror and say what ails him, I'll listen and say nothing more. The phone buzzes and Phil focuses his anger on me. "Arit, pick up your phone. Pick it." A discussion on not taking calls to preserve one's sanity eases the tension, as Mrs. Bamidele says she also has difficulty picking the calls of those she loves.

When Phil says goodbye and shuts the door behind him, the elder woman revisits her fury. "That Phil's a cheat o! I'll tell you how. I gave him 8,000 naira to pay the installation guy for the DSTV, àbí? When I spoke to the doctor about how much he paid his DSTV guy he said no more than 5K. He's been taking off the top. I have proof, now! If he needed money, he should say, 'Mummy I need money,' and if I have, I'll give. Don't you agree?"

Phil has his reasons for taking what's not his. He wants to get to Montreal. He's been reeling for the last month because his visa to Finland was denied, and he's late on his car payment because he's been working for the Madam, who by his calculations owes him over 200K, but he'd accept 70k for the month, but doesn't quite know how to ask for this. He's picked a new city to go to, it has fewer immigrants so as not to ruin his chances of getting abroad. "I want to start bringing things from Africa to Canada," he says. "A friend in New York does this and makes good money. Please push for this with Mummy. She knows people in the embassy, sef. I've done all this work like a son would for his mother. I expect this favor."

I've let my Mom know I have a Mum, not to wound her, but to say that this Mum reminds me of someone I could have met. A crass woman that children from good families never talk about when an ocean separates them. Though my grandmas are dead I think one of them behaved as the Madam does. Which means my Mom must have known a woman like her, and I suppose this binds us.

Last night I wrote to her, my friend.

Nkechi,

The letters I write and the prayers I say
are for me.
I share them with no one.
I'm sure that's how our mothers were.
If we read their diaries, we'd uncover
worlds.
They're far more interesting creatures
than us.

P.S.
Do you know how many worlds you
live between?

P.P.S.
The man with the sliding knuckle asks
me when I'll learn how to cook my native
soup.
Says none of what I eat is what my ancestors ate.

Mrs. Bamidele and I go for a walk around the estate, admiring the bush flowers growing in a vacant
plot that nobody tills, they're upright and the petals
are yellow, and the sun hasn't beaten them dry yet.
The sky is turning pink and the outside lights have
switched on.
"So, what about him?" Mrs. Bamidele asked.
"Phil?"
"Who else?"

She had me watching him for a week to answer if he was executive driver material. Could he embody the nature of an executive, stately and reliable?

"What do you think about him?" She asked. The day Phil drove myself, a bank teller, and the Madam to apartment hunt, his entire backside hung out as he pulled a pack of water out of the trunk. A large slit with curly tufts of hair going down the middle of his crack was out for everyone to see. We had all wished none of us had mentioned being thirsty. He and the bank teller took us to a popular shawarma spot next to an open dumpster with flies zipping above. It made me uneasy that there was a random banker taking time out of his schedule to show us around. But if you and the banker are friendly, and you dash him 2,000 naira for a job well done, and you know the banker's home language, and you are a good client who happens to tell him that you're house hunting, the banker may have a contact who can show you some places in Jahi, and this is how you may end up in a car with a random banker.

The Madam muttered, "Jesus Christ of Nazareth," watching Phil wipe his nose on his hand when giving us our shawarmas. From then on she made it my task to watch him.

We turned towards the playground.

"He stole from me, dear," she said.

"He did." I confirmed.

The phone rang again, I had taken it off vibrate. I checked to see who was calling.

"It's her isn't it?" She asked.

"Yes, this time"

"Did you send her those pictures? She needs to see that you're looking spiky."

"I sent them."

"Good. Now call her."

"Will do. Later."

We strolled along, staring at the houses with the largest gates. Some had barbed wire coiled at the top, some stretched up into the sky, the highest ones had dogs crossing back and forth inside the premises, barking at those passing. If anyone got too close, they would stick their nose between the metal poles and snarl. The men in charge of guarding the houses sat in plastic white chairs outside the gates, listening to the radio, not troubled by the yowling canines. If I had my notepad, I'd have scribbled:

Nkechi,

   Mrs. Bamidele says America was shown the other side of midnight.

   She asks if it's a democracy or not.

   Gates with barbed wire surround the White House after the riot.

   She says the red, white, and blue, is acting like the Third World.

   In this part of the world it's the aspiration to have large gates closing you out.

As we trudged back towards the guesthouse Mum touched my arm to get my attention. I had grown accustomed to her calling my name at least three times in staccato spurts to demand an audience, but this subtle approach was markedly different. "Why punish us for being ourselves?" she asked. "It's no secret our inadequacies abound. But your mother will never stop chasing you. It's not possible."

I gave her a hug and promised to fix tea before I left for the evening. I had found that below her endless preoccupations was a woman who was disheartened. It's this knowing of her that prompts me to send Mom all the pictures she asks for, but I can do no more than that, to everyone's disappointment not every child can carry the moon.

The following day I find a message reading:

My dear daughter,

Maybe you'll visit where my grandma had her garden if it's safe for you to go?
You look good.
God guide you, give you wisdom, and protect you.
I love you very much.

I have doubts about what world I should prioritize above all the others. I could forget about dancing with the ancestor girl, but then I'm not sure I would have been able to develop the sharp eye needed when riding okadas, or when making sure the roasted yam with the red sauce is cooked well. And then there are those hidden worlds smothered against my mother's chest that have set everything into motion. I can see her as a girl eating eben. It doesn't grow where she lives now. There are thousands that nudged her to love this fruit, just as those same thousands nudged me to love a good soup with eba, though I always thought I'd end up loving something else. I've come to know that the thousands are as close to me as breathing, not as close as God, but as near as putting on a shirt and feeling it rub against you, they are always brushing against us, and still I'm unsure if this is a bond or a binding.

In my dreams I've received a new visitation, from a very old woman, so wrinkled her face looks like a tree. She must be family because she smiles with all her teeth just like my mother, that is when my mother allows herself to smile. Her hair is long and gray. She says no one else but God can hear us, and I wonder what God? Hope it's not the jealous God, the autocratic God, or the White God, because I listen to none. "I hope you don't mind," she says. The very old woman says she's been wanting to tell me a message to edify me in the years to come:

> Life is a dance of humans traversing in and out of worlds, until the Maker says you have done what you need to do. With constant change, it is guaranteed that worlds will collide.

I could have grabbed her and squeezed her, as I had been directed to do before, or woke up the next morning and called the pastor to send me back into my dream with the thatched broom to sweep her away, but instead of doing that, I leaned closer in and said, "Continue."

Acknowledgments

Bola Labinjo
Tobi Ogunna
Ann Meredith Wootton
Amy Sass
Aroji Otieno
Gloria Amodeo
Karen Lowry
SA Sanusi
Shemiye Bala
Rita Osakwe
Gloria Amodeo
Dylan Perese